Mrs. MacGregor

Lillina looked at the brownies admiringly, but she didn't take one. "I have to watch my figure," she explained. "I'm going to do some modeling when I go home this fall." She took a dainty sip of lemonade.

Caroline swallowed a brownie in four bites. "Tell me about your problem," she coaxed. "Your husband, I mean."

She ate the rest of the brownies while Lillina talked. It turned out to be the most romantic story Caroline had ever heard — better, really, than a soap opera, because it had happened to this girl who was just a few years older than herself.

Other books by
BETTY REN WRIGHT

A Ghost in the Window
Christina's Ghost
Ghosts Beneath Our Feet
The Dollhouse Murders
The Secret Window
Getting Rid of Marjorie

THE SUMMER OF MRS. MACGREGOR

Betty Ren Wright

AN
APPLE
PAPERBACK

SCHOLASTIC INC.
New York Toronto London Auckland Sydney

Scholastic Books are available at special discounts for quantity purchases for use as premiums, promotional items, retail sales through specialty market outlets, etc. For details contact: Special Sales Manager, Scholastic Inc., 730 Broadway, New York, NY 10003.

ISBN 0-590-41052-0

Copyright © 1986 by Betty Ren Wright. All rights reserved. Published by Scholastic Inc., 730 Broadway, New York, NY 10003, by arrangement with Holiday House. APPLE PAPERBACKS is a registered trademark of Scholastic Inc.

12 11 10 9 8 7 6 5 4 3 2 1   8 9/8 0 1 2 3/9

Printed in the U.S.A.   01

First Scholastic printing, June 1988

For Stella Williams Nathan

Chapter 1

When Caroline's mother was frightened, her freckles popped out and she looked no older than her daughters.

"Linda's worse," she said. "It's just like the last time — those awful bluish places under her eyes — " Her voice broke, and she put a hand to her mouth, a familiar gesture that meant talking didn't help. "This room is an absolute mess, Caroline."

Caroline Cabot looked around, startled. Her completed miniature rooms, each in its own box, were stacked against one wall. School notebooks were heaped on the floor next to the desk, ready to be packed away for the summer. She couldn't stack them on the desk because the floor plans for a dollhouse were spread out there, where she'd left them last night. Next to the desk, a newspaper-covered cardtable held carefully carved bits of wood, scraps of cloth, tubes of glue, an Exacto knife, and a box of tiny tacks. The room didn't look messy to Caroline, just pleasantly used.

"I can't clean it up now," Caroline protested. "I'm right in the middle of — " She stopped. It was no use describing the rocking chair she was making. Her mother had crossed to the window and was staring blankly into the bright June sunshine.

"Go in and talk to her, will you?" Mrs. Cabot said, as if Caroline hadn't spoken. "Tell her she must eat. She'll never get stronger if she doesn't eat."

"Okay." Caroline longed to comfort her mother, but she didn't know how. There was something about that rigid, grieving spine that always made Caroline feel clumsy and stupid. She hurried out of the room, pausing for a moment in front of the hall mirror. *You're not really invisible, dummy,* she told herself. *It just feels that way.*

She took a deep breath and turned toward the big corner bedroom that was her sister Linda's. Sunlight met her at the door. It glowed through organdy curtains and lay in bands across the pale rose carpet. It sparkled off the crystal bottles on the dressing table and turned Linda's blond curls into a halo against her pink pillow. The room held sunlight the way a fishbowl held water. It was the perfect Linda-type room, Caroline thought for the thousandth time. Blue jeans and

T-shirts, gluey fingers and shaggy hair didn't belong here.

Not that her sister wasn't always glad to see her. "Hi," she said now, and lifted one thin hand in greeting. "You're just in time, Carrie. You *like* chicken noodle soup. You can have this — all yours, free of charge."

"Eat it yourself." Caroline crossed to the bed and curled up at its foot. "Mom'll feel bad if you don't. She likes her daughters fat. Look at me."

"You're not fat," Linda said. "You're just right for twelve." She slid the soup bowl across the footed bed tray in Caroline's direction. "I honestly can't swallow it," she said. "I can't! Please, Carrie?"

Caroline squirmed.

"Just this once. You're a lifesaver," Linda added.

"I'm a garbage can," Caroline said, but she picked up the bowl and drank the broth quickly. Then she ate the chicken and noodles, putting the spoon back in the bowl after each bite in case their mother came in unexpectedly.

While she ate, she studied her sister. Linda had lain back against the pillows and closed her eyes. She looked like a porcelain doll propped up in the center of the wide bed. She had a doll's golden hair and too-white skin. *Looks like an angel and acts the way she looks.*

That was what Joe, their stepfather, always said about his older adopted stepdaughter, pretending to tease but meaning every word of it. No one could refuse Linda anything for very long, and Caroline was sure that would be true even if her sister weren't seriously ill. Linda was the kind of person people loved without question and wanted to please.

The long-lashed eyes opened. "What are you staring at? What's wrong?"

"Nothing. I was just thinking."

"Mama's worried, isn't she? I can tell."

Caroline shrugged and looked guiltily at the empty soup bowl. "She just wants you to eat. I'm supposed to be encouraging you right now."

"You tried," Linda said. Her fingers twisted the rose-sprigged sheet. "I couldn't get my breath last night," she said in a low voice. "I was afraid to go to sleep because I might stop breathing." She reached up to the headboard and clutched Teddy D. Bear, who always sat next to her pillow. For a moment, she buried her face in his scruffy tummy and hugged him, as if she were five instead of fourteen. "It was awful, Carrie. I was so scared."

Caroline felt her own color draining away at the thought of not being able to breathe. "You should have called us," she scolded. "Why didn't you?"

Linda lifted her face from the teddy bear. "What could you do? What could Mama do? Or Joe? I'll have to go back to the hospital again — I know it." She sounded much older and like someone else, not gentle, uncomplaining Linda. "I've done nothing but lie here and rest for months, and it hasn't helped. I'm going to die, Carrie. Nobody wants to say so, but it's true."

"No!" Caroline struggled to keep panic out of her voice. "It's not true! You just had a bad night. . . ."

Quick footsteps sounded in the hall, and Mrs. Cabot came in. Her face was set in the smile-mask she always wore in this room. Caroline wondered if Linda guessed how quickly the mask slipped away outside the door.

"Now, how are things going in here?" At the sight of the empty soup bowl Mrs. Cabot clapped her hands, a single sharp clap. "Wonderful!" she exclaimed. "I think your appetite is picking up, sweetie."

Caroline pretended to see something interesting out the window. Linda picked up her milk and took a sip to make up for cheating on the soup.

"What are you two going to do today?" Mrs. Cabot demanded. "It's the first day of Caroline's vacation — let's plan something special." Caroline thought of birthday parties where you were expected to have a good time even if you'd much rather be home reading a mystery.

"I don't think — " Linda began in a small voice.

"I can pick up a new movie at Video Fair. What would you like to see? And Carrie can make popcorn — doesn't that sound like fun? An old-fashioned movie-and-popcorn afternoon."

Caroline looked at Linda. She was as white as the milk in her glass, and her lips trembled, as if all that forced enthusiasm exhausted her.

"I was going to work on the rocking chair I started last night," Caroline said. "It's the last piece for the family room. And then I'm going to weave a little rug."

"Well, Linda can help you." Mrs. Cabot sounded as if this was an even better idea than her own. "We can bring the card table in here, and the two of you can have a great time — "

"No," Linda interrupted. There was something so definite, and so sad, in the single syllable that Mrs. Cabot stared at her in dismay.

"I can't *do* anything, Mama. My chest hurts and it's hard to breathe. I just want to lie still."

Mrs. Cabot's smile slipped. Then it righted

itself, and she leaned forward to touch Linda's forehead. "I think I might call Dr. Krieger," she said casually. "We haven't checked with him for a while, have we? Not that there's anything to worry about, but I'm sure he'd want to know if you're *especially* tired."

Caroline expected Linda to protest, but her sister lay quietly, eyes closed, as if she'd stopped listening. Mrs. Cabot hurried from the room.

"Now I'll go back to the hospital," Linda said in a low, flat voice. "That's what Dr. Krieger will say."

"Maybe not," Caroline whispered. *Cheer her up, dopey*, she thought. *Say the right thing for a change.* "You don't know for sure that you're worse."

"I do know," Linda said, her eyes still closed. "It's okay, Carrie. And thanks for eating the soup."

Though the day was as warm as midsummer, the paramedics wrapped Linda in two blankets. Still, she trembled with cold. Caroline stood stiffly next to the stretcher. She wanted to bend down and whisper good-bye, but she didn't do it. There were too many nosies watching from their front yards and picture windows.

"All set, beauty?" Joe had rushed home

from the plant when he heard the news. He touched Linda's forehead with his fingertips, like a priest giving a blessing. "Mom's going to ride in the ambulance with you, honey, and I'll be right behind in the car. Don't worry about a thing."

Linda nodded to show she'd heard.

"I'll ride with you, Joe," Caroline said. But he shook his head and pulled her out of the way so the paramedics could lift the stretcher into the ambulance.

"You stay here and call your aunt Grace, kiddo," he said. "And Grandma Parks. We don't want them to hear about this from somebody else. Better give the Martins a call, too."

Mrs. Cabot came running down the front walk, clutching her handbag, a sweater, and Teddy D. Bear. She scrambled into the ambulance and crouched on the floor, her face close to Linda's.

"There's a bench you can sit on," Caroline called, just before one of the paramedics climbed in and slammed the door. The other man ran to the driver's seat, and the ambulance swung away from the curb, with Joe's battered blue sedan right behind it.

Caroline stood on the sidewalk, watching the red lights signal *trouble trouble trouble*, listening to the siren slice up the quiet of Barker Road. When she turned away, finally, the neighbors were returning to their own affairs. The house seemed to have changed in some subtle way, so that she dreaded going back inside.

"Hold it, *please*. This will make a terribly moving shot." The rich, gravelly voice spoke from behind her. "It'll have everything — grief, loss, loneliness. If you could see yourself, dear, you'd know what I mean."

Caroline whirled around. Who would dare talk like that — as if she were just *pretending* to feel bad — when she was hurting so much? Years later, she would recall that moment and the fiery explosion of anger that wiped away despair, at least for the moment, and marked her first glimpse of Mrs. Lillina MacGregor.

Chapter 2

She was at least a head taller than Caroline, and very slim. Her skirt was palest lavender, her blouse was white, and a sprig of purple lilac was pinned in her copper-red hair. Most of her face was hidden by the camera she pointed at Caroline.

"Cut that out!" Caroline, who never made scenes, was shouting. It felt good. Shouting was better than crying, and she'd been very close to tears a minute before. "I don't want my picture taken!" she roared. "Who are you, anyway?"

The camera came down. The girl raised elegantly arched eyebrows. She looked surprised but not angry. "That *was* rude of me, I suppose," she said after a moment of thought. "It's just that when an artist sees so much raw emotion . . . Forgive me, little one."

"Little one!" Caroline's voice squeaked

with outrage. "I'll be thirteen in October. How old are *you?*"

"Seventeen. And I'm quite old for my age. When you've lived a lot, age doesn't mean a thing." The girl smiled, a dazzling smile that lit her tilted brown eyes. "My name is Lillina Taylor MacGregor, by the way," she said, and advanced on three-inch heels to hold out her hand. *"Mrs.* MacGregor. What's yours?"

Caroline gritted her teeth. "Caroline Cabot," she said, trying for cool dignity. *"Miss* Caroline Cabot."

"I suppose they call you Carrie."

"Caroline. My name is Caroline." She'd never shaken hands with another girl before, and she felt as if the neighbors must all be back at their windows, watching. "I have to go in," she said. "I'm supposed to make phone calls."

"Of course, dear. You run along." Lillina touched her long, shining mane. "What's wrong with whoever-that-was in the ambulance? Your sister? Is she going to be all right?"

Caroline shivered. It was not a question she wanted to think about, certainly not one she wanted to discuss with this irritating stranger. "She has a weak heart. Sometimes she has trouble breathing and she has to go to the hospital. My father — my real father —

had the same sickness. He died when we were small. That's all I know." She bit off the words, then discovered to her astonishment and confusion that there were tears in Lillina's eyes. Caroline saw her own pain reflected in the slanty eyes as clearly as if she were looking into a mirror.

"That's really dreadful," Lillina said. "Caroline, if you'd like me to come in with you for a while, I can spare the time." She laid a hand along one narrow cheek. "Actually, you'd be doing me a favor. My skin is so incredibly delicate, and I've been out taking pictures for hours."

Caroline hesitated. She dreaded going into the empty house alone, and most of her anger had dissipated at the sight of those unexpected tears. Still, there was something disturbing about this girl. She talked like — like a film star, maybe, or a member of the jet set. And she asked nosy questions.

"The thing is," Caroline said, "I don't really know you. Just your name."

Lillina nodded, as if she approved of this kind of caution. "I'm practically a neighbor of yours, dear," she said. "For the summer, anyway. I'm a house guest of the Restons. Mrs. Reston is my aunt Louise. She's a darling, isn't she?"

Caroline pictured large, square-jawed Mrs. Reston. She wore her hair in a crown of tight braids, and she had a loud, no-nonsense voice. "Darling" was not a word Caroline would have chosen, but it didn't matter. Mrs. Cabot liked her.

"You can come in if you want to."

It was a cool invitation, but Lillina didn't seem to mind. She followed Caroline through the front door, looking around with an odd hunger.

Caroline pointed to the living room. "You can sit in there," she said. Then she slumped into the chair in front of the telephone niche in the hall and dialed her grandma Parks.

Grandma cried. She cried hard, and Caroline knew she was thinking that it had been only three months since the last trip to the hospital. "I'm sorry, Grandma," she said. She watched Lillina so she wouldn't cry herself.

The living room was two steps lower than the rest of the house. It had always seemed to Caroline a good way to break your neck if you weren't expecting the steps, but she knew her mother loved the sunken living room. Lillina loved it, too. She paused at the first step and pointed her toe. Then she put out her hand as if someone were waiting to kiss it, and she sort of drifted down the steps. Her spine was very straight and her head was high, and when she turned she was wearing a haughty little smile. Caroline blinked and blew her nose, impressed in spite of herself. Lillina looked like Miss America about to receive her crown.

Aunt Grace was next on the list to be called, and Caroline had to listen while her aunt ranted about the Cabots wasting time and money at the local hospital when they should be going to the Mayo Clinic or to some other big, important medical center. Caroline reminded her, as politely as possible, that Linda had been taken to the Mayo Clinic two years ago, and the doctors there had said Grand River Hospital was doing all that could be done for her. Joe always said Aunt Grace refused to believe that some things couldn't be changed. He said she believed that if you did thirty sit-ups every morning, ate enough fiber, and voted Republican, you'd live forever.

The Martins weren't home.

By the time Caroline had completed her calls, Lillina had made her way all around the living room. She'd examined every vase, lamp, and trinket, stopping for a full minute to study the gray-brown sandpiper huddled on the coffee table. When she came back up the steps to the hall, she looked at Caroline with the same concentration.

"It's so strange," she murmured. "That little bird makes me think of you, for some reason."

"The sandpiper? What do you mean?"

Lillina looked back at the bird again. "My parents have this marvelous beach house," she said. "I simply love the sandpipers there — they are my favorite birds. They're timid, of course, but they can take care of themselves beautifully. They dash about through the waves, doing what they want to do, and they don't pay any attention to the big seagulls bustling around. They're really smart — and independent!"

Caroline decided not to be insulted. "Where do you live when you're not at the beach house?" she asked.

"New York. Manhattan, to be exact."

"You *live* in New York?"

Lillina picked up her camera and pointed it in the direction of the sandpiper. Then she put it down on the telephone table again. "That's right," she said. "Our apartment is at the top of one of the tallest apartment buildings on Fifth Avenue. I'm just visiting the Restons for a few weeks this summer. My mother and Mrs. Reston were best friends at school, and when the difficulties began — about Frederick, that's my husband — they decided I should spend the summer here. Not that I minded terribly, you see. After the initial pain of being separated from Frederick, I knew it was the best solution to the whole problem."

A half-hour before, Caroline had been sure she'd spend the rest of the day moping in her room. At this very moment, Grandma Parks was crying and Aunt Grace was muttering to herself, and awful things were being done to Linda in the hospital. Yet Caroline was beginning to feel almost cheerful. She couldn't stop asking questions, even though she'd been annoyed with Lillina for doing the same thing.

"What kind of problem?" she asked. "Are you really married?"

Lillina flashed a stunning smile. "Really and truly. I'll tell you about it, if you want to listen."

Caroline wanted to, very much. "Would you like some lemonade?"

"Delightful, dear," Lillina said. "I really think that in warm weather lemonade is more satisfying than champagne, don't you?"

"Yes," Caroline agreed, "I do," though she'd never tasted champagne in her life. Dazedly, she led the way to the kitchen, where Lillina perched on a stool. Caroline opened a can of lemonade concentrate and mixed it with water in her mother's best pitcher. After a moment's hesitation, she brought out a plate of brownies she'd baked for Joe.

Lillina looked at the brownies admiringly, but she didn't take one. "I have to watch my figure," she explained. "I'm going to do some modeling when I go home this fall." She took a dainty sip of lemonade.

Caroline swallowed a brownie in four bites. "Tell me about your problem," she coaxed. "Your husband, I mean."

She ate the rest of the brownies while Lillina talked. It turned out to be the most romantic story Caroline had ever heard — better, really, than a soap opera, because it had happened to this girl who was just a few years older than herself.

"You mean your mother and father forced you to leave Frederick?" she asked, her mouth sticky with chocolate. "On your wedding day?"

Lillina nodded. "When you put it that way it sounds cruel, but my parents are marvelous people, Caroline. They admire Frederick very much — he's an absolutely marvelous person, too — that's why they gave us permission to get married in the first place. But at the wedding my mother began to cry and tell everyone I was too young to be married and Frederick was too old for me."

"How old is he?"

"Thirty-five. I've always loved distinguished-looking older men. At first, Frederick tried to argue with my mother. He reminded her of all he intends to do for me — he's very wealthy — and he told her how much we meant to each other. But it was no use. My poor dear mother became absolutely hysterical."

Caroline scooped up the crumbs from the brownie plate. She tried to picture herself in love with a distinguished-looking older man and her mother becoming absolutely hysterical. "So what happened then?"

"We talked it over and decided on a compromise." Lillina stretched her long body gracefully and smiled. "My mother said I ought to go away for a while, and Frederick finally agreed. He said he didn't want to spoil my excellent relationship with my parents if a few weeks would make that much difference to them. He said he would have the builders start our house in Connecticut while I was away, and everything would be ready by this fall." She shrugged and took another sip of lemonade. "And so here I am in Wisconsin," she said. "It's difficult being separated, of course, but the Restons are lovely people. And as long as I have my camera, I can work on my portfolio. I'm going to start accepting picture assignments as soon as I get my portfolio together." She put her glass back on the table. "That's why I wanted those pictures of you after the ambulance drove away. You have a very expressive face, Caroline — just what a professional photographer looks for."

Caroline's cheeks felt hot. Was "expressive" the same as "pretty"? Probably not, but it was a pleasant thing to hear about yourself. This girl was nice as well as different.

Caroline began hoping that her problem would keep Lillina MacGregor in Grand River for a long, long time.

Chapter 3

"I didn't know Louise Reston had a niece," Caroline's mother said. They were eating in the kitchen — hamburgers and French fries bought on the way home from the hospital, and a bowl of alfalfa sprouts because Mrs. Cabot had decided they had to have a salad even if she was too tired to make one.

"Lillina isn't her real niece," Caroline explained. "She's the daughter of Mrs. Reston's best friend. They live in New York. Lillina just calls Mrs. Reston Aunt Louise because it's more respectfully intimate than plain Louise."

"Good for Lillina." Mrs. Cabot's eyes crinkled briefly as if she'd heard something funny. "Anyway, I'm glad she kept you company till we were able to call. You'll have to ask her to come over to play again — now what's the matter?"

"Lillina's too old to play. So am I."

"Well, pardon me, I'm sure." Mrs. Cabot stretched and rubbed her eyes. "Anyway, I'm glad you have a new friend. And now I'm going to call the hospital, and if everything's all right I'm going to bed. I've never been more tired in my life."

"Good idea," Joe agreed before Caroline could point out that it was only a little past eight. "You get a good night's sleep, hon. Carrie and I'll clean up."

Joe, lumbering around the kitchen, looked even more tired than Caroline's mother. He was six foot three, with a hard chin and an Indian-chief nose and bushy eyebrows. His hair was gray, though he was only thirty-eight, and his shoulders were massive even when they sagged. It was hard for Caroline to talk to Joe, because she loved him so much and because she was a little afraid of what he might say to her. He believed in speaking the truth at all times, even to kids. The truth could be hard to listen to.

She gave her mother time to get to her bedroom. "Is that all the doctor said?" she asked then, trying to sound casual. "That there's a new medicine he wants to try?" She'd felt secrets in the air, all during supper.

Joe pinched the skin above his beaky nose. "He said Linda's weaker than last time. He said there's a heart stimulant that might help, but it's experimental. Your mom's counting on it too much, I'm afraid. And he said Linda should be careful not to overdo."

They glanced at each other, and away. *Overdo!* Caroline thought. *How can Linda do less than she's been doing? She might as well be dead.*

She dropped that thought fast.

"One more thing," Joe said, finally getting to the secret part. "If we go ahead with the new medicine, it can't be done here. Linda would be part of an experimental program at a clinic in Boston. She'd have to go there." He rubbed his nose again. "Your mother would go with her."

"For how long?"

"A couple of months, I guess."

Caroline knew it was all settled. Her mother would say they were going to talk it over and make a Family Decision, but if the trip might help Linda, the decision was already made. Caroline could look ahead to a whole summer alone, with Joe at work every day and the house as empty as it had been this afternoon.

"What a lousy business!" Joe growled. "Here's a kid who has the sweetest personality on this earth, and she has to go through so much trouble. What's right about that? I'm asking!"

Caroline knew he didn't really expect an answer from her. Even the minister had a tough time with that one, and Joe asked him about it every time he came to call. *What's right about that?* It seemed their lives moved in circles around the question. Even when no one asked it, it was there, because Linda was there and feeling miserable. How could bad things happen to a perfect person? How could God make such a mistake?

Later, while Joe called Grandma and Aunt Grace to tell them what the doctor had said, Caroline went outside. There was a fresh summer smell in the darkness, and the moon looked like a neon-lit Frisbee. She wondered if Linda could see the moon from her hospital bed. And then she wondered why she wondered. Sometimes it seemed she couldn't have a single thought that didn't involve her sister.

Footsteps approached — the sharp click and long scrape of high-heeled pumps that kept slipping. The sidewalk curved fifty feet north of the Cabots' house, so Caroline couldn't see Lillina at first, but she knew who was coming. Who else on Barker Road would go for a walk in high heels?

When Lillina appeared, her head was thrown back and she was staring at the moon. Her arms were extended behind her, and she seemed to trail moonlight from her fingertips.

"Speak to me, O night goddess," she chanted. "Fill me with your beauty." She froze, a graceful, moon-washed statue, and

Caroline held her breath. The strange, silly words had charged the night with an eerie tension. But nothing happened. Lillina waited for a moment, then turned up the Cabots' walk. She didn't seem the least embarrassed when she saw Caroline sitting on the step.

"Have you found my camera, dear?" she asked. "I think I left it here this afternoon."

Caroline jumped up and opened the screen door. The camera waited on the table next to the telephone. She'd already planned to take it over to the Restons' house first thing in the morning if Lillina didn't return for it.

"Thank heaven," Lillina said huskily when Caroline returned. "I couldn't bear to lose it. Just a few more shots, and I'll have my portfolio ready to send to *Vogue*."

She wasn't really skilled enough to take pictures for a big magazine. She couldn't be. But Caroline felt a thrill of excitement in spite of herself.

"It's not your camera, it's Mr. Reston's," she said, trying not to sound accusing. "His name's on the tape at the bottom."

Lillina blinked. "So good of him to let me use it," she said vaguely. "I left home in such a mad hurry. . . ."

Caroline swung the camera away from Lillina's outstretched hand. "Promise you won't show *my* picture to anyone," she demanded. "Promise!" She'd been thinking it over, and she'd decided she didn't care how expressive her face was. Red eyes, puffy face, tangled hair, scruffy jeans — that was what people would see in the picture Lillina had taken that afternoon.

She'd expected an argument, but Lillina just smiled. "You can trust me, Caroline. I always get a subject's permission before I release a picture."

Caroline held out the camera. As she did, moonlight glinted on the little window at the top. It was empty.

"Hey, there's no film! You forgot to put film in the camera." She could hardly believe it. How could a person who expected to be a professional photographer forget a thing like that?

Lillina's smile hardly quivered. "Actually, you're right," she said. "But I didn't forget, dear. I don't always choose to use film. I may spend a whole day just filling my head with images. It helps me to grow as an artist. You've heard of pianists practicing their fingering on a paper keyboard, haven't you?"

Caroline hadn't. She felt as if she'd been the butt of a joke. "That's crazy," she said. "No film!"

Lillina took the camera and sat on the step. "Artists do unusual things, but that doesn't mean they're crazy," she said. "How is your sister, Caroline?"

The surge of outrage faded. Lillina sounded genuinely concerned. Caroline realized that several minutes had passed since she'd thought about how bad everything was.

"Linda's going away," she said, and she repeated what Joe had said about the experimental medicine and the clinic in Boston.

When she finished, Lillina's tilted brown eyes were thoughtful. "I'm sorry," she said. "I guess you'll be awfully lonesome for a while."

"Don't be sorry for *me!*" Caroline exclaimed. "You should be sorry for Linda. She's the one who's sick."

"I'm sorry for both of you."

"Listen," Caroline was exasperated, "it's a lot worse than you know, Linda having this sickness. She's a really special person." She knew this to be true; she'd heard it at least a hundred times from Joe, the truth-speaker. And her mother agreed, even though she hugged Caroline and said *every* person was special in her own way. If Caroline were the sick one, she knew her parents would be sorry, but for Linda to be sick was worse. "When Linda could go to school, she always got straight A's. And she was Sleeping Beauty in the all-school play. Her picture was on the front page of the *Grand River Herald.*"

"She sounds marvelous," Lillina murmured. She looked at Caroline thoughtfully. "Are you interested in the theater, too?"

Caroline rolled her eyes. "No, I'm not," she snapped. "The best part I ever had in a play was in second grade. I was the bush the wolf hid behind until Red Riding Hood came down the path." She grinned in spite of herself, and Lillina laughed, a warm, husky sound.

"Well, my sister Eleanor and I are nothing alike either," she said. "She doesn't have my unusual coloring, or my height. She won't make a model, but she's charming in her own way."

Caroline sniffed. As if everyone in the world wanted to be tall and thin and red-headed! She was torn between wanting to hear more about Eleanor and wanting to make Lillina see how tragic Linda's illness was.

"I didn't know you even had a sister," she muttered. "How old is she?"

"Thirteen in July. A wonderful child. Of course," said Lillina, unaware of the waves of irritation shimmering in the night air, "dear Eleanor has some abilities I don't have. She's terrifically talented in math, for example. I wouldn't be surprised if she was the next Einstein." She doubled up, chin on knees, and pulled at tufts of grass. "What's *your* thing, Caroline?"

"I don't have a thing."

"Of course you do. What do you like to do the most? What do you want to do in the future?"

Caroline tucked a wisp of hair behind her ears. Building dollhouses and miniature furniture sounded pretty childish compared to Eleanor's terrific ability in mathematics. She would tell Lillina about that some other time, not now. "I want to go to England," she said. "By myself."

"You mean when you grow up?" Lillina stopped her grass-pulling.

"No, I mean this year. At Christmas." Now that she'd said that much, she might as well tell the rest. "My friend Jeannie Richmond lives right outside London. Her dad was transferred to England last year, and they'll be there for another year. We were best friends before she went away. My grandma Parks says she'll buy me a round-trip ticket, if I can save up a hundred dollars for spending money. That's all I'd need because I'd stay with the Richmonds."

She jumped as Lillina abruptly unfolded her long self and pirouetted across the lawn. "But that's marvelous, Caroline!" she cried. "I love it! I simply adore it! You're going, of course."

"No way." Caroline wished she hadn't started this. "Do you know how much money I have in the bank? Seventeen dollars and seventy-three cents. Even if I saved my whole allowance this summer, I wouldn't have anything like a hundred dollars. And I can't save every darned penny!" Miniature furniture kits were expensive.

Lillina dropped down on the step once more. "Get a job," she commanded. "Earn tons of money!"

"I'm twelve years old!"

"You can baby-sit. Or run errands for people. Or clean houses." Lillina paused. "I don't suppose you write," she said. "That can be very profitable. When I finish my novel, I'm sure I'll make more money than I'll know what to do with. But a novel takes time, of course."

Caroline didn't challenge her. What was the use? A person who could tell you to earn money by either running errands or writing a novel wasn't going to be bothered if you said she wasn't making sense.

The trouble was that Lillina's enthusiasm was stirring up all the excitement Caroline had originally felt when Jeannie's invitation arrived two months ago. The dream trip even began to seem possible. People on Barker Road took care of their own children or enrolled them in day-care centers. And no one that Caroline knew was likely to hire her to clean house. But there *was* something she could do to earn money. It would be dreadful, but she supposed she could do it if she had to.

"Why exactly do you want to go to England?" Lillina broke into her thoughts. "I mean, you said your friend will be back here in a year."

"I just want to go." Caroline pressed her lips together and stared into the night. Lillina could ask all she wanted, but Caroline wouldn't let herself be pushed into answering that question. She hoped that God Himself didn't know the real reason, it was so ugly. How could He love a person who wanted to get away from her sick sister? How could He care about a sinner who longed to do something — anything! — that her sister would never, never be able to do?

Caroline was annoyed again, with herself and with Lillina. "I have to go in," she said. "It's getting late. Besides, you'd better go home. You could be attacked or something, standing around in the dark talking to the moon."

She knew how mean she sounded, but Lillina's smile was forgiving. "You're like my darling Frederick," she said. "He worries about me constantly." She shook her head over some secret thought. "Of course, the person you're really like is my sister Eleanor. The similarity is amazing."

"Like her how?" Caroline demanded. "*I'm* not good in math."

"Well, you look a lot like her," Lillina replied. "And I'm sure you have special talents of your own. Actually, you're the way Eleanor *used* to be — before she got herself together." She narrowed her eyes, as if trying to decide whether to go on. "You both have this special problem to overcome, of course. But if Eleanor could do it, I'm sure you can, too."

Caroline glared at Lillina's calm profile. What in the world could this girl know, or think she knew, about Caroline's problems? "What do you mean?" she snapped. "You hardly know me."

Lillina smiled warmly and sweetly. "But I know you and Eleanor both have older sisters, dear. Older sisters who" — she dropped her eyes modestly — "well, nobody's perfect, I suppose, but it's easy to *think* your older sister is perfect when you admire her so much. And it's ever so hard to be your own best self when you're always wishing you were like someone else."

Caroline jumped up. Trembling with rage, she had to fight back an impulse to push this infuriating girl right off the step.

"That's DUMB!" she shouted. "That's the dumbest thing I ever heard!"

"No, it isn't," Lillina said softly. "It's the truth." She stood up and touched Caroline lightly on the wrist. "You really *must* go to England, dear," she said and strode down the walk, pausing at the curb to raise a hand and wiggle her fingers in farewell.

Like a sophisticated model.

Or a best-selling novelist.

Or a world-famous photographer.

"La-de-da," Caroline grumbled and stomped into the house.

Chapter 4

"Mr. Jameson!" Linda was disbelieving. "You can't work for *him*, Carrie. Everybody says he's a terrible crab!"

Caroline made a face at herself in the mirror over Linda's dressing table. She often made faces at herself, particularly when she and Linda were reflected side by side.

"It might not be so bad," she said. "I mean, what can he do except yell at me? And order me around? And tell me how stupid I am!" She shuddered and ran across the room to fling herself on the pale pink comforter covering Linda's bed. "Oh, I'll hate it!" she moaned. "And you'll be gone. And Mom will be gone. And Joe will be at work all day. There'll be nobody to talk to. . . ." She stopped, out of breath, and waited for her sister to say something.

When she looked up, Linda was still at the dressing table, picturebook pretty in the rose-colored suit their mother had bought for the airplane trip to Boston. She was looking in the mirror and frowning.

"It'll be bad for you, I guess," she agreed. "Maybe even awful. But I'd rather do that than go to Boston. Mr. Jameson would be better than — oh, you know. . . ."

Better than blood tests and hospital trays and feeling weak all the time and having shots and not being able to breathe at night. Caroline rolled over and stared at the ceiling. *I never think of anyone but me! I only told her about my job because I want her to feel sorry for me. How can I be so rotten? All I have to do is help a sick old man for a few hours every day, and then I can come home and forget about him and do whatever I want. While Linda has to lie there all day in that dumb hospital . . .*

"I'll write you about it," Caroline said unhappily. "You can read my letters and then tear them up and be glad you're a long way off so you don't have to listen to all the complaining in person."

"What complaining?" Mrs. Cabot appeared at the door, crisp and smiling. "What in the world do *you* have to complain about, Caroline?"

"Her job," Linda said. "I think she's really brave to do it."

"Do what? What job? What on earth are you talking about?"

The girls exchanged a glance, and Linda mouthed, "I'm sorry," into the mirror.

"I was going to tell you before you left, Mom," Caroline explained hastily. "Mr. Jameson asked Joe if I would work for him this summer, remember? There's a nurse who comes for a couple of hours early in the morning and a housekeeper who comes at about four to clean up and make dinner. But he needs someone in between to run errands and pick up papers that fall on the floor and look for things that get lost and . . . stuff. It'll just be for a couple of hours every day. I told Joe to tell him this morning that I'd do it."

Her mother looked distracted, and Caroline knew that in her mind she was already on the plane, speeding toward Boston. She didn't want to hear about complications at home.

"As I recall," Mrs. Cabot said, "you told Joe when he mentioned it the first time that you'd rather die than work for Mr. Jameson. You said you wanted to keep as far away from him as possible. Am I right?"

Caroline nodded.

"What's happened to change your mind?"

This would be the worst possible time to remind her mother of Grandma's promised ticket to England. Caroline knew that both her parents considered her too young to make such a trip by herself. Probably the only reason they'd allowed Grandma Parks to make the offer was that they were sure Caroline couldn't, or wouldn't, save a hundred dollars before Christmas.

"Well, I just changed my mind. Why shouldn't I work for him?" She knew she was whining, but she couldn't help it. "I have to have *something* to do all summer."

For just a moment there was a flicker of cold anger in Mrs. Cabot's eyes that made Caroline cringe. It said, very clearly, that Caroline had no right to whine when her wonderful sister was so sick.

And she's right, Caroline groaned inwardly. *I absolutely hate me.* She wished her mother and Linda were already on their way to Boston so she could be miserable by herself.

"Well, do what you wish." Mrs. Cabot shrugged the subject away. "I just can't imagine you sticking with it very long, though. I hear that poor old fellow is really a bear. I know he's sick and unhappy, but there are other people who are sick, too, and they manage to remain sweet-tempered." She darted across the bedroom and gave Linda a hug. "Are you ready, honey? Aunt Grace is going to pick us up in about five minutes to take us to the airport."

Caroline decided it was time to disappear. Aunt Grace approved of the trip to Boston — "getting to the bottom of things," she called it — but she did not approve of Caroline's staying home alone while Joe was working. "Caroline can come with me to Madison," she'd announced, as soon as she heard the plan. "She can go to summer school at the university while I'm taking classes, and in our free time I'll teach her how to crochet."

Caroline's mother had actually hesitated for a moment, but Caroline's frantic expression had helped her make up her mind. "That won't be necessary," she'd said. "Thanks, anyway. Caroline will find plenty to do here — she always does — and she and Joe can keep each other company in the evenings."

Aunt Grace had argued, but Mrs. Cabot remained firm. Caroline knew it was as much for Joe's sake as her own — he was going to be lonely — but she was grateful. A whole summer with Aunt Grace was a numbing thought.

"I'm going out," Caroline said. "Right now."

Linda grinned, and Mrs. Cabot said, "Good idea." She put her arms around Caroline and kissed her soundly. "Be a good girl, dear," she said. "Help Joe all you can."

"I will," Caroline promised. She returned

her mother's hug and then kissed Linda's pale cheek. "You answer my letters or else!" she threatened. "Tell me everything."

"I won't have anything to tell," Linda said. She put thin arms around Caroline and clung to her as if she hated to let go. Caroline saw tears on her sister's face as she moved away. She rubbed her own wet eyes with a fist and hurried down the hall, through the kitchen to the back door.

The day was warm. Gray woolly clouds wandered across a gray-blue sky. Caroline walked to the end of the yard and edged around Joe's white-painted toolshed. Between the back of the shed and the Kramers' tall redwood fence was a four-foot strip of lawn, as precisely trimmed as all the rest of the yard because Joe was that kind of gardener. This was Caroline's private place, her hideaway. She flung herself full-length on the grass and pillowed her face in her arms. The hazy sun's warmth settled like a blanket on her shoulders.

I wish I could stay here all summer. It was a silly thought, but she meant it. She imagined herself sailing off the edge of the world, as if this patch of lawn were a magic carpet. Her mother and Linda were far below her (car door slamming, Aunt Grace's bright, abrasive voice), and Mr. Jameson was a black dot on his front porch. She drifted across oceans of sky, away from school friends (scattered for the summer, anyway, at camp or on vacation with their parents), away from guilt feelings and loneliness. She imagined Lillina MacGregor on the carpet beside her, taking pictures over the side. *This is marvelous, Caroline,* she'd say. *I wish dear Eleanor were here with us.*

Eleanor. Caroline sat up, and the magic carpet became grass again. It was more than a week since Lillina had said Caroline and Eleanor were a lot alike. She began to think she'd like to know Eleanor better — Eleanor, who had already overcome her "special problem."

Caroline decided she wanted to see Lillina again and tell her about the job with Mr. Jameson. It was, she was sure, the kind of undertaking Eleanor would admire.

For some reason, that made the whole idea a little less horrible.

Chapter 5

"You're absolutely right, of course," Lillina said. "Nursing is practically Eleanor's thing. I think it's what she wants to do with her life."

"You said she was going to be a famous scientist like Albert Einstein." The girls sat on the Cabots' front steps watching the Kramer boys and Joey Millikan race their bicycles down Barker Road. Lillina had appeared a half-hour after Caroline returned from her hideaway and wandered through the empty house. Linda's sun-filled bedroom had depressed her; without Linda in it, it was like a furniture display window, pretty but unused. Her own room was no more welcoming; it seemed dreary, and she wasn't in a mood to work on her miniatures. She went into the dining room and took an apple from the bowl in the middle of the table. She was at the telephone, looking up the Restons' number, when she heard high heels clacking and scraping along the walk. Caroline felt as if she'd summoned a genie out of a bottle.

"Well, she does very well in math," Lillina agreed. "But what she really wants is to help people. The thing about Eleanor is this: she can probably do anything she wants to do. She seems like such a quiet little thing, but inside she's *very* strong."

"I wish I could meet her," Caroline said wistfully. "I wish she'd come to visit the Restons, too."

For a moment Lillina looked sad. Then her chin lifted, and she ran a hand over her shining red hair. "So do I," she said softly. "But our parents would be all alone then, and that would be dreadfully hard on them. The four of us have always had such marvelous times together." She shaded her eyes with a slim, freckled hand. "Is that the man?"

"Who?"

"You know. Your patient."

Caroline followed her stare across the street. Mr. Jameson had opened the front door of his bungalow, and he was clinging to the door frame as he looked up and down the street. When he saw Caroline, he swung one arm in a clumsy, impatient gesture, nearly losing his balance in the process.

"That's him." Caroline's heart sank.

"What's he acting so angry for? I'm not supposed to go over there until ten o'clock."

The old man waved again, and his lips twisted in a grimace. Caroline fought an impulse to run into the house and lock the door behind her.

"I suppose I'd better go," she said. "Maybe his clock's wrong. Do you want to come along?"

Her friend shook her head. "I absolutely must get back to my novel. And I want to do some portrait shots of Mrs. Reston this afternoon. As a special favor. Besides" — she turned away from Caroline's pleading expression — "I might make him uncomfortable. You know?"

"Uncomfortable!"

"I suppose it sounds silly, but some people ... I'll meet your Mr. Jameson another time."

"He's not *my* Mr. Jameson. I've never even talked to him." Caroline's knees shook as she stood up and brushed the seat of her pants. She crossed the street, feet dragging, Lillina's odd comment lingering in her ears.

"You're younger than I thought. About ten, ain't ya?"

Up close, Mr. Jameson looked nine feet tall. He was dark and wrinkled, with bony temples and big wrists. His eyes were black and bright, with little folds of skin drooping over them.

"I'm nearly thirteen."

Mr. Jameson's expression said he doubted it. "Don't know if you can be of much use, after all. Better forget the whole thing. Go play with your dolls."

Caroline felt her face redden. She was fired — before she'd even stepped inside Mr. Jameson's front door!

"I'm strong," she said, in a voice that was louder than she meant it to be. "I can work real hard." She sounded unconvincing to herself, whiny, close to tears.

The old man squinted down at her like an eagle on a treetop. For a moment he clung, swaying, to the door frame; then the black eyes glazed and he took a step backward.

"Well, come on in, if you want to," he muttered. "No use standing out here all day."

He reached for a table in the small entranceway and rested his weight on it. Then he clutched the frame of the door leading into the living room and pulled himself ahead, one shaky step at a time. Caroline held her breath as he crossed the room, grasping chair backs, and lowered himself into a straight-backed chair in front of a television set.

She wondered what to do next. The living room was small and filled with overstuffed furniture that looked as if no one sat on it. There were crocheted covers on the arms of the sofa and crocheted mats on the little tables. Mr. Jameson's chair and the television set, in the middle of the flowered carpet, looked as if they didn't belong there.

"Don't stand behind me!" The old man's strength, and voice, seemed restored, now that he was sitting down. "You one of them sneaky types, always going around on tiptoe?"

This was so unfair that Caroline didn't even try to answer. She moved in front of the television screen.

"Do you want me to work for you or don't you, Mr. Jameson?" She tried to be mature and reasonable, but the words had a quavery, pathetic sound. "I'll go home if you say so."

Mr. Jameson ignored the question. "You ain't the beauty of the family, are ya? That sister of yours — the sickly one — she got the looks. Used to see her out playing when she was on her feet."

She wouldn't cry, if that was what he was waiting for. Time enough for that when she was alone. "I'm going home," Caroline said.

Mr. Jameson looked at her with contempt. "Easy enough to walk away," he said. "Well, suit yourself. I don't care what you do. An old man is nobody in this world. Nobody! Go on home — you'd just be in the way around here."

Caroline started toward the front door. She pictured herself telling people what Mr. Jameson had been like. Linda would be sympathetic. Her mother would say, "I told you so." And Lillina — Lillina would say, "How dreadful for you, dear. Of course, Eleanor would never have given up."

Mr. Jameson twisted in his chair and glared over his shoulder, his lined face contorted with rage and — something else. What was it? Satisfaction because he'd hurt her enough to make her leave? Yes, that. And fear! Caroline's eyes widened. He was afraid. He was afraid that an old man really was nobody in this world.

She recognized that fear. She knew what it was like to look in a mirror just to make sure you were still there.

"I guess — I guess I'll stay for a while," Caroline said. Cautiously, she returned to her position in front of the television set. "Do you want to write a letter or anything?" she asked. "I can do it for you." That was supposed to have been one of her chores.

Mr. Jameson looked triumphant. "Nope," he said.

"Should I make you some coffee?"

"Ain't thirsty."

"Do you want me to run some errands?" She waited for another refusal.

He stared down at his slippers. "Need peanut butter," he mumbled. "Couple of chocolate bars. Maybe a crossword puzzle book." He refused to meet Caroline's eyes. "Money's in the kitchen. The tin can on the shelf next to the sink."

Caroline took a long, uneven breath. She had a job after all.

The kitchen, like the living room, was old-fashioned and spotlessly clean. In one corner stood a walker, the kind Grandma Parks had used for a while after her hip surgery. Caroline found the can containing a few bills and some change and took out three dollars and some quarters. Then she picked up the walker and carried it back to the living room.

"Why don't you use this?" she asked, setting it close to Mr. Jameson's chair. "Then you wouldn't have to hang on to the furniture when you move around."

A big fist lashed out, and the walker flew across the room.

"That's what I think of the blasted thing!" he roared. "I'm not a cripple! You mind your own business!"

Caroline darted out the front door. He'd actually thrown the walker — not at her, perhaps, but close enough to scare her badly. Her mother was right. Mr. Jameson was a bear — a mean, nasty-tempered bear who hated everybody because he'd been hurt himself.

Stepping into the sunny quiet of Barker

Road was like returning home from a far-off, unfriendly land. Caroline considered going home for her bike but decided to walk the three blocks to the Super-Saver instead. She certainly wasn't in any hurry to get back.

The Restons' neat, gray-shingled bungalow lay beyond the second curve. She hesitated in front of it, then turned up the walk. Lillina was probably busy, but the walk to the Super-Saver wouldn't take her away from her book for long. And since Caroline and Eleanor were supposed to be so much alike, it would be interesting to find out from Lillina what Eleanor would do if Mr. Jameson were *her* employer.

The house had a closed-up look, but Mrs. Reston came quickly when Caroline rang the bell. Her aproned figure filled the doorway.

"Caroline! How are you, dear? Did your mother and Linda get on their way all right?" Her voice boomed a welcome, but her face was flushed and her smile seemed forced.

"I'm fine. They left at nine o'clock." Caroline answered the questions in order. "I was wondering if Lillina could walk to the store with me. If she isn't too busy, that is."

Mrs. Reston's smile vanished. "I'm afraid she can't come out right now," she said. "She's in her room. We're having a little problem that has to be straightened out before she does anything else."

Caroline was incredulous. "But she was at my house this morning. You mean she's *grounded?*" Grounding happened to kids, not to a married woman from New York City.

"Well, something has come up." Now Mrs. Reston sounded definitely unhappy. "It's not a matter I want to go into, dear. We'll get it straightened out, I'm sure."

The smile returned, and Caroline knew she was expected to leave. Still she lingered, trying to get used to the idea of a grounded Lillina. Maybe, she thought, Mrs. Reston was one of the people whom Lillina made uncomfortable. Maybe she was kind of jealous because her own two daughters, both grown up and married, were just ordinary people, nothing like Lillina.

"I'd better go," Caroline said. "Would you please tell Lillina — "

"Lillina?" Mrs. Reston interrupted. "Why do you keep calling her that? Is that what she told you her name is?"

Caroline nodded.

"Well, her name is Lillian, dear. Not that a name matters, of course. She is what she is. And I'll be glad to tell her you stopped by." Mrs. Reston glanced over her shoulder and lowered her voice slightly. "I'm so glad you've befriended her, Caroline. She needs a nice, down-to-earth friendship, I'm sure."

Caroline left, feeling that she'd been in-

sulted enough in one morning to last a life-
time. And Mrs. Reston hadn't even been
trying!

Nice.

Down-to-earth.

Nobody.

She began to run. She ran all the way to the
Super-Saver, and then she ran all the way
back, speeding up as she passed the gray
bungalow where Lillina was grounded. Not
that she was eager to get back to Mr.
Jameson-the-bear, of course. But running
was better than walking when you didn't
want to think.

Chapter 6

Caroline expected to see Mr. Jameson at his front door as she rounded the corner. But the door stood open, just as she'd left it when she'd run away, and the old man wasn't in sight. She slowed to a walk and went up the steps on tiptoe. *Figure out what good old Eleanor would do*, she told herself, heart thudding. Pretend the earlier, bad scene hadn't happened. Do whatever work Mr. Jameson would let her do. Try not to get into an argument.

She peeked into the living room. Mr. Jameson was fast asleep in front of the dark television screen. His cheeks sagged in heavy downward lines, and his eagle face looked softer in sleep.

Caroline carried her purchases out to the kitchen and looked around. What could she do? The morning nurse had washed the breakfast dishes before she left. She tiptoed down a little hall to the bedroom. The bed was made, but a dresser drawer stood open, and a comb lay on the floor. She put the comb on the dresser cloth and closed the drawer. The bathroom was neat, except for a towel that had slipped off the rack. *I don't know what he needs me for, anyway*, Caroline thought. She went back to the kitchen. Might as well go home and have lunch.

Lunch! That was something she could help with as part of her job. She took the peanut butter from the Super-Saver bag and tiptoed around the kitchen finding bread and milk. There was a bowl of fresh fruit on the counter, and she thought briefly of adding a banana to the peanut-butter sandwich, then decided against it. If Mr. Jameson didn't like the combination as much as she did, he'd probably claim she was trying to poison him. She set the sandwich plate and the milk on a tray and added a little jar of jelly (everybody liked jelly with peanut butter, didn't they?). A polished apple served as dessert.

When she returned to the living room, Mr. Jameson was still asleep. His chin almost touched his chest, and he had begun to snore. She moved one of the little end tables close to his chair and put the tray on it. As an after-thought, she laid a chocolate bar next to the plate.

The walker was on its side against the sofa.

Caroline picked it up and started back to the kitchen with it. Then she changed her mind. When he woke up, the lunch tray would let him know she'd decided to forgive — or at least ignore — his earlier meanness. But she wasn't wrong about the walker. If he didn't use it, he was almost certainly going to fall. She set the walker at his side and tiptoed out quickly, easing the screen door shut behind her.

She wanted to be a safe distance away before he woke up.

Mrs. Cabot called soon after Joe came home from work. She sounded cheerful, but Caroline wasn't fooled. A new treatment, a new doctor, a new diagnosis always meant a period of hope. A week from now — or a month — if she was still optimistic, that would be time enough to cheer.

"How was the job, Carrie? Is Mr. Jameson as difficult as people say?"

"He was okay." Caroline wasn't going to spoil her mother's good mood. "He was about the way I thought he'd be."

Mrs. Cabot chuckled. "That bad? And you're going back tomorrow?"

"Oh, sure." Caroline wondered whether Mr. Jameson would even let her in.

They talked a while longer, and then it was Linda's turn on the phone. She sounded tired;

to her, a new treatment just meant more pain, more long hours in a hospital. But she had a nice roommate almost exactly her own age, and the food at the clinic was better than the food at Grand River Hospital. They were going to have Hawaiian chicken tonight, and one of the aides had promised that if they ate everything on their trays she would demonstrate how to do a hula. She wasn't Hawaiian, Linda explained, but she was taking dance lessons at a YWCA.

"Wish I could be there," Joe said. He was on the bedroom telephone, so that he and Caroline could both hear everything that was said.

"We wish you were here, too," Linda said wistfully. Caroline realized how hard her sister was trying to sound cheerful for her family's sake. She wondered if Joe was fooled.

He wasn't. When they had said good-bye and he returned to the kitchen, his face was grim. "That poor kid," he said. "I wish I could go through this for her. It's so darned unfair." He switched on the oven and opened the freezer. "There're five different casseroles in here. You care which one we have tonight?"

"No."

He sighed. "I'm sorry I forgot to ask you how it went with old Jameson today. Was he really okay?"

Joe looked so tired and depressed, Caroline

decided she couldn't confide in him either. "He doesn't have a lot for me to do," she said. That much was true.

"You going to keep on going over there?"

"I — I don't know. If he wants me. If there's enough work."

"Good for you." He wandered back to the refrigerator and stood looking into it as if he couldn't remember why he was there.

"Mom left a twenty-four-hour salad in there," Caroline said helpfully. "Your favorite kind."

"Sounds fine." He closed the door and settled heavily at the kitchen table with the *Grand River Herald*.

Caroline went outside. What a strange, unsettling day it had been! First, saying goodbye to her mother and Linda. Then the terrible meeting with Mr. Jameson. And then the peculiar conversation with Mrs. Reston. What was the mysterious problem that was keeping Lillina grounded in her room? And what was her real name, for goodness' sake?

Without really deciding to do it, Caroline walked down Barker Road to the Restons' house. A radio or television played softly inside, but Lillina didn't appear. Maybe, Caroline thought, the problem was so bad that Mrs. Reston would send Lillina home to New York. The thought was surprisingly painful.

She tried ESP. *Come on out, Lillina-Lillian.*

I want to talk to you. I need to talk to you.
She stood there for a few minutes, until she began to feel self-conscious. Lillina wasn't coming, and that was that. Mrs. Reston wouldn't let her.

There was nothing to do but go home to the casserole and the fruit salad and lonely Joe.

Chapter 7

"It was nothing," Lillina said. "Aunt Louise and I just had a tiny misunderstanding."

"It didn't sound so tiny," Caroline protested. "She said you had to stay in your room until the problem was settled."

Lillina shrugged. "Actually, I had a delightful day," she said firmly. "I need time alone occasionally. To meditate."

They were lying in Caroline's hideaway place behind the toolshed. Lillina wore a bikini. She was so thin that the scrap of cloth forming its top stretched handkerchief-flat across her chest. Her hips were as narrow as a boy's. Still, it was clear from the way she lay there, ankles crossed, arms curved above her head, that she felt as beautiful as any cover girl in a swimsuit.

Caroline decided to try once more to get at the truth. "But what happened yesterday?

You're not going back to New York right away, are you?"

Lillina gave her a startled glance. "Of course not, dear," she said. "I just arrived in Grand River, after all. Even my darling Frederick would be shocked if I came home right now. He wants our house to be nearly completed and ready for furnishing when I return." She smiled dreamily. "There's going to be a sunken living room, did I mention that? And a darkroom where I can develop my pictures. And a simply marvelous study. My desk will be in front of a window where I can look out over the rose garden. Did I tell you Frederick wins prizes for his roses?"

"No, you didn't." Caroline waited, hoping for more details about yesterday's tiny misunderstanding, but Lillina seemed to have forgotten all about it.

"Your aunt Louise says your name isn't Lillina," Caroline said, after a short silence. "She said it's Lillian."

Lillina lifted herself on one elbow and cocked an eyebrow. "Lillian, Lillina," she repeated mockingly. "Do you know, she actually accused me of lying to you, until I showed her this." She plunged a hand into the oversized shoulder bag lying next to her on the blanket and handed Caroline a worn scrap of paper. It was a birth certificate, folded twice and falling apart at the creases, but very authentic-looking.

"Lillina Jane Taylor," Caroline read aloud. She was surprised at how relieved she felt to know Lillina hadn't lied.

"Elizabeth Taylor, the movie star, is my father's second cousin," Lillina said. "We invited her to our wedding, but she was in Europe making a film. Anyway, the point is, that's my birth certificate, and you can see for yourself that Lillina is my name." She took back the paper and folded it carefully away. "People called me Lillian when I was a child, but I knew they were wrong. The first time I saw my birth certificate I said, 'There, that's the real me.'"

"I don't understand," Caroline said. "How could you — "

"Aunt Louise says someone made a spelling mistake on the certificate." Lillina laughed that idea away. "Lillina is my *true* name. You believe me, don't you?"

Caroline nodded, fascinated. "How about your mom and dad? What do they call you?"

"Whatever I want them to. My parents are very understanding. My mother always says, 'Be the person you want to be, dear. Express yourself.'" Lillina looked at Caroline speculatively. "Haven't you ever wanted to change your name?"

"I'd rather change me and keep the same

name," Caroline replied. Her name was one of the few things she liked about herself.

Lillina smiled. "Now that's exactly the kind of thing Eleanor would say. Eleanor is changing all the time. Improving herself, I mean. You really are so much like her, it's remarkable."

Mention of Eleanor brought Caroline back to thoughts of her job. This morning she'd watched Mr. Jameson's nurse help him from the house and into a waiting cab. When she'd crossed the street at ten o'clock, there had been a terse note tacked to the front door: *Mr. J. has a doctor's appointment. Come tomorrow, same time.* So he still wanted her to work for him. Maybe he'd liked waking from his nap and finding his lunch prepared. Or maybe he'd just decided it would be fun to have someone to throw things at whenever he felt like it. In any case, Caroline was glad she didn't have to tell people the job had ended after just one day.

"I started working for Mr. Jameson yesterday," she said, trying to sound offhand. "That's why I stopped at your house. I was going to tell you about it." She paused.

"Marvelous," Lillina murmured. "You should get a nurse's uniform right away. You'll look stunning in white."

Caroline glanced down at her faded blue T-shirt and cut-off jeans. "I don't look stunning in anything," she said flatly. "Besides, I might not be working for Mr. Jameson very long. He's really crabby."

"Mmmm." Lillina rolled over on her stomach and yawned. "You'll be all right," she said lazily.

Caroline opened her mouth to describe yesterday's experiences, then changed her mind. She was disappointed that Lillina seemed interested only in the uniform.

"Is he going to pay you lots of money?" Lillina asked, after a while. "How long will it take to earn the one hundred dollars?"

Caroline didn't want to admit that she and Mr. Jameson hadn't discussed payment. "It won't take too long, I guess," she said, hoping she was right. "Anyway, it beats baby-sitting."

That, at least, was the truth. The one time Caroline had been a sitter, she'd been asked to substitute for the Kramers' regular sitter who had come down with flu. It had been for only two hours, and since Caroline was barely a year older than the oldest Kramer boy, and since they had spent the time playing games together and watching a detective show, the Kramers had decided that it was more a visit than a job. They had sent her home with a stack of the boys' old comic books and a piece of cake from the birthday party they'd attended. Joe said she ought to complain, but Caroline couldn't make herself go back to ask for money. It was easier to despise herself for letting people walk all over her.

"I used to adore baby-sitting when I was young," Lillina said. "I'd make up little plays, and the children would act them out. They always wanted me to play the fairy queen." She smiled at the memory. "Your sister Linda and I have quite a lot in common, don't you think? Of course, I've never met her, but you've told me so much about her. She was Sleeping Beauty in a school play, you said. It's quite a coincidence, really, since you're so much like *my* sister and all."

Caroline gaped at her. Lillina, stretched in the sunlight like a skinny, contented cat, felt as beautiful as Linda really was. How *could* she feel that way, when she wasn't even pretty? Unusual — that's what she was — not pretty.

"My legs are starting to burn," Caroline muttered because she couldn't think of a way to disagree without sounding mean. "Let's go in and make some lemonade."

Lillina sat up. "I have a better idea," she announced. "Let's go to the shopping mall, Caroline. Why lie around here when we could be having an adventure?"

Caroline made a face. "Going to the mall is

no big deal," she said. "Besides, I don't have money to buy anything, and I hate just wandering around."

"We won't wander," Lillina said. Her brown eyes sparkled, and she was as wide awake as she'd been sleepy moments before. "Come on, Caroline, let's do it. You get into one of your little dresses, and I'll go home and change. I'll meet you at the bus stop."

"A dress!" Caroline protested. "We don't have to wear dresses to go to the mall. But you can't wear your bikini," she added hastily, because she suspected Lillina might be capable of just that. "You'll have to change if you really want to go."

"We both have to change," Lillina insisted. "No shorts, Caroline. You'll see, we'll have a terrific time."

Caroline felt uneasy. She wished she knew what Lillina had in mind.

"Dressing up to go to a shopping mall is dumb," she said, but the argument was already lost and she knew it. Lillina stood up, unfolding her long length gracefully and smoothing her hair. "I'll bring my camera," she said, as if determined to deepen the mystery. "This should be a perfect opportunity."

Opportunity for what? Caroline decided it was no use asking. "Put some film in the camera this time," she said sourly and went inside to find a dress.

Chapter 8

Marquette Mall spread out over several acres, like a gigantic cream-frosted wedding cake. Bright-colored flags whipped and snapped a welcome above the south entrance as the girls stepped down from the bus.

Lillina sparkled as brightly as the flags. All the way across town she'd chattered about how much she liked to shop, what a spectacular wardrobe she'd left behind in New York, and how she hoped some day to own a store that sold high-fashion clothes. That would be her first investment, she said, after she became rich and famous.

Now, as they approached the mall, she seemed almost breathless with anticipation. Caroline was excited, too. She had smoothed back her dark hair and fastened it with one of Linda's gold barrettes. Her dress was a dark blue cotton with a white collar. Her mother said once that it looked like a uniform, but Caroline liked it. It was plain and neat, and when she wore it she didn't expect anyone to tell her she was stunning. Because she wasn't.

Lillina had seemed a little disappointed when they met at the bus stop. But then she'd said, almost at once, that Eleanor had a dress cut very much like Caroline's, in shades of gray and brown.

"A sandpiper kind of dress?" Caroline suggested shyly.

"Exactly! You're a darling pair of sandpipers, and I'm a — "

"Peacock," Caroline said. She looked admiringly at Lillina's bright costume — a long, gold-colored cotton skirt with the white blouse she'd worn the first time Caroline saw her. There were at least six colored chains looped around her throat, and her hair was combed back behind her ears, held in place on one side by a yellow tulip from the Restons' garden. Sunglasses, huge and sequined, almost covered her narrow face.

As soon as they were settled on the bus, Lillina had tugged at the blouse to make it settle lower on her shoulders. "Oh, Caroline, this is fun!" she exclaimed. "I haven't been shopping for ages."

"I don't like to shop," Caroline said. "Usually. Does Eleanor like it?"

"Not unless we go together." Lillina tugged

again at the blouse until the elastic neckline threatened to snap. "Then she has a wonderful time."

Now, as they entered the cool, brightly lit mall, Lillina walked right past the stores that offered clothes for juniors. There were at least six shops that Caroline's friends always visited; their racks were crammed with jeans and pants and tops. Lillina acted as if these places weren't even worth her notice. Though she hadn't been to the mall before, she seemed to know what she was looking for. When they reached Margo's Fashions, the most expensive shop in all of Grand River, she turned in at once.

Caroline followed. She'd never shopped in this store, even with her mother. The creamy carpet, silvery walls, the peach-colored sofas made her think of a stage set. There were no customers except for a stout man, sunk deep into one of the sofas, who looked bored to death and kept shooting impatient glances toward the dressing-room door in the rear of the store.

"You can't shop *here*," Caroline whispered. "You'd have to have about a million dollars — "

"It doesn't cost anything to look, dear." Lillina moved slowly around the store, pausing in front of one elegantly dressed mannequin and then another. When a saleswoman appeared from the dressing room, she didn't retreat or act embarrassed.

"May I help you?" The saleswoman looked as if her girdle was too tight and her shoes were too tight and her glasses pinched her nose. She examined Lillina carefully as she approached. Caroline realized then why Lillina had insisted they dress up. If they'd been wearing jeans, they would probably have been ignored by this imposing lady. They might even have been asked to leave.

"That's a charming little thing you're looking at," the saleswoman said. "Perfect for summer evenings."

Lillina shrugged carelessly. "Sweet," she murmured. "But not for me."

Now she'll tell us to get out, Caroline thought. She took a step toward the front of the store before she realized the saleswoman was smiling.

"Well, then, what did you have in mind?" she asked. "We have some marvelous things that have just come in."

"Something in black linen, I think." Lillina said the words slowly, looking around the store as if she doubted she could be satisfied. The man on the sofa had stopped watching the dressing-room door and was staring at Lillina instead.

Caroline fought an attack of nervous giggles. She wanted to run away almost as much as she wanted to see what was going to happen next.

"Let me see what we have. Some of our new gowns were just unpacked and pressed this morning." The saleswoman excused herself and hurried away.

"Now what?" Caroline whispered. "She thinks you're going to try something on, Lillina!"

Lillina thrust Mr. Reston's camera into Caroline's hands. "I am," she said. "I *love* trying on clothes. And I need some pictures for my model's portfolio. That'll be your job, Caroline. Wait until the clerk is looking the other way and then take my picture."

"I can't. She'll see the flash!"

"Not if you're quick. I'll tell you when. There isn't any flash."

Lillina turned away quickly as the saleswoman came back carrying several dresses over her arm. She held them up for inspection. Two were black, one a sea-green cotton that would look wonderful with Lillina's red hair, and the fourth a pale yellow.

Lillina shook her head at one of the black dresses but nodded approval at the other three. "I really don't *need* another green," she said, "but that shade — "

"Perfect for you, of course," the saleswoman said. "Just perfect. I know you're going to love it." She led Lillina to the dressing rooms, walking faster now, as if her shoes didn't hurt quite so much.

Caroline felt a quiver of guilt. All her friends tried on pants or tops once in a while; their favorite stores expected it and encouraged the customers to put things on layaway if they couldn't afford to buy right away. But this was different. The saleswoman didn't know Lillina was playing a game. She was trying to be helpful, and they were wasting her time.

Behind one of the mannequins, out of sight of the man on the sofa, she examined the camera. It was much like her mother's, except that her mother's model required flashbulbs. She focused on one mannequin and then another, until voices sounded from the dressing room and another clerk appeared with a heavyset woman customer behind her.

"Nothing looks right," the woman snapped at the man on the sofa. "I'm so disappointed. I'd really hoped . . ." Her husband heaved himself out of the couch and followed her from the store, hardly seeming to hear her complaints. Caroline noticed that he looked back once. She guessed he was sorry to leave before Lillina reappeared.

"Well, what do you think?"

Caroline swung around to the dressing-room door. A stranger stood there — a tall, sophisticated stranger in a simple black sheath. The yellow tulip and bright-colored chains were gone. The fall of red hair swung forward and partly covered one slanted brown eye.

Lillina laughed at Caroline's expression and pirouetted across the carpet. It was the same graceful dance she'd done the night Caroline told her about her dream trip to England. *If I tried that*, Caroline thought, *I'd fall over my own feet and break an ankle.*

"You look terrific, Lillina." It was the no-nonsense truth.

"She does, doesn't she?" The clerk's cheeks were pink with pleasure. "Of course, the white sandals are all wrong. And I think the neckline could take some simple jewelry. Let me get some pearls and we'll see. . . ."

She bustled off, and Lillina gestured swiftly toward the camera. "Now!" She settled on the arm of a sofa, tucking her feet to one side so the sandals didn't show. Then she tipped her head back and smiled. Caroline snapped a picture.

"Now this." Lillina narrowed her eyes and looked haughtily amused. Caroline peered through the finder. Her fingers trembled. *She's beautiful*, she thought. *She really is like Linda, after all.*

Twenty minutes later, Lillina had tried on all three dresses, and Caroline had taken pictures of her in two of them. The yellow one was last, and in Caroline's opinion it was the loveliest of all. But the saleswoman didn't give her a chance to take a picture. In fact, her manner had changed slightly, and she seemed faintly puzzled as she watched Lillina strike a pose in front of a three-way mirror.

"Just how old is your sister?" she asked Caroline in a low voice. "I assumed she was —"

"She's not my sister," Caroline mumbled, suddenly panicked.

"What do *you* think, Caroline dear?" Lillina threw the words over her shoulder without looking away from her reflection. "Actually, I'm rather fond of all three of them, aren't you? But I don't dare take them all. Frederick would be furious. Unless, of course —" She turned to the saleswoman. "Do you know, I believe I'll have my husband come in with me. He enjoys picking out my clothes, and he has such definite tastes. . . ."

The clerk's face flushed with resentment and weariness. *She knows*, Caroline thought. The excitement of the last half-hour began to fade fast.

"I'll meet you at the fountain," she mumbled as Lillina turned back to the dressing room. The clerk glared, and Caroline almost ran from the store. She didn't want to be there when Lillina promised again that

Frederick would come in to look at the dresses.

"You know he can't come," Caroline accused a few minutes later when Lillina joined her at one of the upholstered benches near the fountain. "He's hundreds of miles away. Why didn't you just — "

"Say I didn't like the dresses?" Lillina smiled. She had a shining look. "Do you think she would have believed that? She knew I loved them all."

"Well, I don't think she believes you're married either," Caroline said. "She was beginning to act kind of funny. I think she knew you weren't going to buy anything."

"It was just *fun*, Caroline. After all, that other customer didn't buy anything either."

"That was different."

Lillina looked as if she were tired of this conversation. "Actually, I could buy at least one of those dresses if I really wanted to. Frederick is going to send me money every week or so. Anyway" — she hugged herself — "now I have some more pictures for my portfolio, and that's important. A model has to have a good portfolio of pictures to get started. I really appreciate your help, dear." She pulled Caroline to her feet. "No more dresses today," she promised. "I know something that'll be just as much fun."

She whirled away toward the entrance of Bradens' Department Store. Reluctantly, Caroline followed. *But no more dresses*, she told herself. *And no coats or bathing suits or lingerie, either.* It had been thrilling to watch Lillina turn into a glamorous sophisticate, but there was something dishonest about what they'd done. She thought of what Joe would have said if he'd seen them in Margo's Fashions, and her face burned.

Bradens' was crowded. Sale signs hovered over every clothes rack and counter. Lillina moved purposefully through the clusters of shoppers. The yellow tulip had been left behind in Margo's dressing room, but the red hair was easy to follow.

When they stopped, at last, they were in front of a jewelry counter. Not the cheap-costume-stuff counter, Caroline noted sinkingly. Lillina was peering down through the top of the glass case to where more expensive pieces were displayed.

"Look," she said. "That bracelet with the green stones. Like emeralds. Isn't it gorgeous?"

"Mmm." Caroline preferred the plain gold bracelet next to it, but she could see why Lillina liked the green. It was her color — one of them.

"Do you want to try it on?" The clerk was no more than eighteen, a plain, sharp-featured girl who eyed Lillina as if she were some weird, exotic bug.

No! Caroline almost said it out loud, but Lillina was already nodding yes. "I guess I will." Casual again, indifferent, Lillina couldn't hide the quiver of excitement in her voice. She laid a freckled arm on the black velvet display cloth and let the clerk fasten the bracelet in place.

"It looks too heavy for you," the clerk said bluntly. "Too old, too."

Lillina's eyes glittered. "Do you think so?" she murmured. "Then I'd better try on some others."

In rapid succession she pointed out the gold bracelet Caroline had admired, an intricate copper circlet, a wide silver bracelet set with a single agate, and a band of silver dotted with sparkling red stones. Lillina tried on each one, holding out her arm for Caroline to admire, then laying the piece aside with a little shrug.

Caroline shifted from one foot to the other. "I guess you can't make up your mind," she offered, for the clerk's benefit. "Maybe we can come back some other time. . . ."

She started to back away, but Lillina ignored the hint. "The thing is," she said, when there were nine or ten bracelets spread out in front of her, "if I take the red and silver, I'll want earrings to go with them. You do have earrings to match, don't you?"

"I don't know." The clerk sounded cross and a little desperate. "I just work here part-time, so I don't know the stock real well. And I'm not supposed to have this many items out of the display case at once. I'll have to put some of them back."

Lillina looked shocked. "But I haven't decided yet," she protested. "If you'll *please* ask someone about the earrings . . ."

The clerk bit her lip. "I'll ask," she said sullenly. "Just a minute."

As soon as she turned her back, Caroline clutched Lillina's arm. "You're not really going to buy one, are you? That silver bracelet costs fifty dollars, Lillina."

Lillina frowned at the display in front of her. "I just don't know," she said. She picked up the bracelet set with green stones and draped it lovingly over her wrist.

Caroline had had enough. "I'm going to get a Coke," she said. "I'll meet you out in the mall, okay?"

Lillina nodded absently. "I wonder which one Frederick would like best," she mused.

Caroline fled.

They met again at the fountain. Caroline handed Lillina a Coke and took a sip of her own. "I have to go home," she said. "My step-father will be back from work, and he'll wonder where I am."

"If you say so, dear," Lillina said. She seemed different now, still tiptoe-excited, but nervous, too. "Maybe we can come back later this week."

"I'll be working for Mr. Jameson." Caroline didn't want to come back to the mall with Lillina, not for a long time.

"Oh, I forgot about your job." Lillina spun around in one of her little dance steps, almost spilling her drink. "Well, we had fun, didn't we?"

"Some of the time," Caroline replied soberly. "But some of it was like lying, Lillina."

"That's silly, dear. You mustn't be stuffy about things."

Stuffy! Caroline felt put down. She sighed and switched to a more agreeable subject. "You looked great in those dresses — like a movie star. I wish I could do that — I mean, I just wish I could *feel* like that."

Lillina smiled forgivingly. "If you want to be a model, you have to stand up straight, Caroline. You slouch. Pretend you're hanging from a hook above your head. Make your neck as long as possible, and keep your arms and legs loose, like a puppet's. Tuck in your chin. Smile a lot." She crumpled her empty Coke cup and tossed it into a wastebasket. "That's what I tell Eleanor," she said. "Not that she needs much reminding. She has beautiful posture. She isn't interested in modeling, of course, but she has that — "

"Certain something?" Caroline suggested. It was one of her mother's favorite expressions. Linda had that certain something. Lillina had it. Now even a plain old sandpiper-girl like Eleanor had it.

Stand up straight. Pretend you're hanging from a hook. Arms and legs loose. Tuck in your chin. Smile. Tonight, in the privacy of her bedroom, Caroline planned to experiment. It probably wouldn't work, but she'd try.

"We'd better go," she said. "Don't forget the camera." She reached for the camera case and was surprised when Lillina snatched it out of her hands.

"How could I forget it, dear? I mean, the camera is practically my world."

Caroline remembered the day they'd met, and how she'd found the camera lying on the hall table after Lillina had gone home. Maybe that was what the misunderstanding with Mrs. Reston had been about. Maybe the Restons had noticed that Lillina was careless with the camera and they had scolded her about it.

They walked halfway up the mall to the south door and out into the late-afternoon sunshine. "The bus," Caroline pointed at the corner. "We'd better hurry. He might be getting ready to leave."

They ran side by side, Lillina shortening her long lope to match Caroline's shorter stride. They had almost reached the bus when Caroline noticed that the camera was bouncing on Lillina's hip and rattling as she ran.

"Better — fix," she panted. "Camera shouldn't — rattle — like that."

Without slowing her pace, Lillina opened the top of the case and slid her fingers inside. The rattling stopped. They reached the bus and ran up the steps just as the driver grasped the lever to close the door.

"There," Lillina murmured, settling comfortably in the front seat beside Caroline. "Relax. We made it."

But Caroline couldn't relax. The camera case, tucked between her and Lillina, seemed to be burning a hole in her hip.

Had she seen a flash of sparkling green in that second or two that the case was open? *No!* she told herself. *No, I didn't.* But the words sounded false, the way her mother's words sounded when she told Linda she didn't look one bit sick.

There had been something in that case besides the camera. Something that rattled. Something green.

Chapter 9

When Caroline awoke the next morning, her stomach was churning. It was a today-is-the-math-test-and-I-haven't-studied kind of feeling. She lay on her side and watched a narrow finger of sun stretch across her desk to rest on the lampshade she was making from a silver thimble. The lampshade sparkled, and Caroline remembered the reason for this odd, sickish feeling. She'd gone to sleep last night thinking about the glitter of green in Lillina's camera case. She felt as if she'd been dreaming about it all night.

There was a tap on the door. "You said I should wake you." Joe's voice was low and sad-sounding. "I have to leave for work in a half-hour."

Caroline kicked off the sheet. She'd decided last night that she would make breakfast for Joe today. *Bacon and eggs*, she thought as she hurried to the bathroom and splashed cold water on her face. *Cinnamon toast.* She'd never cooked a whole meal by herself, but breakfast shouldn't be hard. Maybe if Joe saw that she was trying to cheer him up, he'd realize how glum, even grumpy, he'd been since the rest of the family had gone away.

The best placemats were on the table, and she was pouring milk when he came into the kitchen. "Well," he said, and Caroline could tell he was pleased. "Didn't know you were into cooking. I thought you didn't get interested in anything that wouldn't fit into a dollhouse."

"I'm interested in food," Caroline retorted. He *was* pleased, even if he showed it by needling her. She put his plate in front of him, and he started eating with enthusiasm, not seeming to notice that the bacon was burned and the eggs were a little dry.

She filled her own plate and sat down opposite him.

"You working for Mr. Jameson today?"

Caroline nodded. "I guess so," she said. "I hope he's in a better mood than he was the first time."

Joe buttered a piece of toast and spooned raspberry jam onto his plate. "I thought you said things went pretty well," he said. "You don't have to do it, you know. He's miserable, poor old guy. He's not used to being dependent on other people, and since he had that stroke he hasn't much choice. Maybe you can't handle it...."

She heard the doubt in his words, the willingness to believe that she couldn't stand up to a difficult situation. "I can do it," she said, with more confidence than she felt. But already, she could tell, he was losing interest in the conversation. Whether she continued her job or not just wasn't that important to him.

"We'll call the clinic in Boston tonight," he said. "Around five-thirty. Your mom will be there to keep Linda company while she eats, and we can talk to both of them."

"Fine," Caroline said. She fought down resentment. He could have been eating his usual cold cereal and instant coffee, she thought. After the first few bites, it hadn't mattered. Linda, far away and too sick to do anything but lie in a hospital bed, was a more interesting stepdaughter than Caroline could ever be.

It was a good thing she had her job with Mr. Jameson to fill her day. She didn't want to see Lillina for a while, or even think about her, and she didn't much want to think about her family, either. Sometimes, when Linda was sickest, Joe would say, "Thank God for my job. If I didn't have a job, I'd go crazy." For the first time, Caroline understood how he felt. She could hardly wait to leave the house.

But a few hours later she wondered how she could have been grateful for a Mr. Jameson in her life. He had gone from difficult to impossible. The doctor he'd seen the day before had roused him to new extremes of temper.

"The fool wants me to give up," he roared. "Wants me to hobble around on that — that thing" — he pointed at the walker — "for the rest of my life! Well, I won't do it. I can walk as well as anybody else. I just need practice." He stood in the doorway between the kitchen and the living room, clutching the back of a chair and rocking dangerously.

Caroline waited until he stopped for breath. "But maybe you should practice with the walker," she suggested timidly. "Just for a while, I mean. Till you get stronger."

Mr. Jameson's answer was a savage kick at the walker. The sudden movement almost sent him crashing to the floor. "You can throw that out with the rubbish, as far as I'm concerned," he snarled, clutching the chair again. "Take it out to the backyard and leave it next to the garbage cans. Go ahead, do it!" He thumped a bony fist on the door frame.

Caroline eyed the walker lying between them. She didn't want to argue and make him more upset than he already was, yet she couldn't do what he asked.

"My stepfather said you wanted me to

write some letters for you," she said. "Maybe we could do that first — if you feel like it."

The rage gradually faded from his eyes as Mr. Jameson considered this suggestion. He dragged himself into the living room and staggered wildly across the carpet to his chair in front of the television set. He sat down and stared for a moment or two at the blank screen.

"All right, then," he said finally. "We can write a letter or two, I s'pose. Got a niece name of Jean in Missouri. Never see her anymore, but she writes. Your handwriting decent?"

"It's okay." Caroline bit her lip. She wasn't going to let him scare her off. She could handle it. *He doesn't really hate me*, she told herself. It was his illness, and his weakness, that made him so short-tempered. She tried to picture what he might have been like before age and illness changed him. Had he been cheerful, straight-shouldered, full of life? She stared, trying to see past the deep wrinkles, the set mouth, and the anger that now seemed part of the old man's personality.

"Pen's in the top drawer of my dresser," Mr. Jameson snapped. "Paper's in there, too. Let's get it over with."

Pleased with herself, Caroline scurried away. She had actually calmed Mr. Jameson in the midst of a tantrum by suggesting something interesting for him to do.

The top dresser drawer held a jumble of pencils, pens, rubber bands, paper clips, and red-and-white mint candies. In the back was an open cardboard box half filled with unmatched sheets of writing paper and envelopes. The paper was yellowed and dusty-looking.

"Hurry up," Mr. Jameson bellowed. "It's all right there — open your eyes."

Caroline took out the top sheet of paper and a wrinkled envelope. She was about to shut the drawer when an edge of dull green, sticking out from under the stationery box, caught her eye. She lifted the box. Dozens of bills — hundreds, fifties, and twenties — were stuffed under it.

She stared at the money. How could Mr. Jameson be so careless! How could he leave all that money in a dresser drawer for a burglar to find as easily as Caroline had found it? Was it possible that he didn't realize how much was there? Maybe he'd meant to take it to the bank a long time ago, or maybe he wanted to take it but didn't know how to get there.

She carried the paper and a pen back to the living room and sat on the couch. "There's a lot of money in that drawer," she said cautiously.

"I knew it!" Mr. Jameson narrowed his eyes at her. "Knew you couldn't help pokin' around."

"I wasn't poking around." Caroline kept her tone neutral. "But what if a burglar — "

"Wouldn't dare," Mr. Jameson shouted defiantly. "I'd brain 'im! Besides, no one knows it's there, and they won't know if you keep your mouth shut. . . . Which, I suppose, is askin' a lot."

He really did want to pick a fight. He was watching her expectantly, and she realized that he'd known she would see the money and had guessed what her reaction would be.

"If you need a ride to the bank, I'm pretty sure my stepfather will take you," Caroline said. *And tell you how dumb it is to keep all that money in the house.* Joe, the truth-speaker, said what he thought to adults as well as to kids.

Mr. Jameson scowled, as if he could hear what she was thinking. "Nobody else's business where I keep my money," he said. "Are we goin' to write that letter or aren't we?"

"Yes, we are." Caroline gave up. She folded some newspapers across her knees to make a writing surface and waited for him to start dictating.

It was a strange experience. Mr. Jameson — bad-tempered, mean-tongued Mr. Jameson — loved his niece very much. Not that he told her so; the way he felt showed more in what he kept to himself than in what he said. He didn't tell her his hands were too shaky to write, just mentioned that a neighbor was helping him with the letter. He didn't tell her he was having a hard time walking or that he'd had to hire a part-time nurse and housekeeper. He didn't complain about a thing. He said he was sorry Jean's husband had lost his job, and he asked about her three children and whether the older boy was still playing in the Little League. He told her not to worry about coming for a visit because he knew she couldn't leave her family. He asked her if she remembered going to the drugstore with him for milkshakes when she was a little girl.

Caroline listened wonderingly. This was a Mr. Jameson she hadn't met before. There was a funny little quiver in his voice when he mentioned the milkshakes, and afterward he sat quietly for a long time, staring at the television screen as if he saw something there that no one else could see.

"How should I sign the letter?"

He looked up, startled. She knew he'd forgotten she was there.

"Sign it 'Uncle Jim.' And get one of them fifty-dollar bills from the drawer."

Caroline signed it "Love, Uncle Jim," and gave him the letter to read. When she came back with the money, he folded it into the letter and tucked it into the envelope. She half expected him to tell her that her handwriting was terrible and that she shouldn't have added the "Love," but he didn't say anything at all.

"I think it's a nice letter," Caroline said. "I bet Jean is going to like it."

He shrugged. "She'll like the money." He looked at her sourly. "Now what?"

"I could fix your lunch."

"Might as well."

"What would you like?"

He made a face. "Doesn't matter," he said. "Same as last time will do."

And that, Caroline thought, *is as close as he'll ever come to a compliment. I guess if he doesn't throw something across the room, that means he likes it.*

After lunch she took the letter to the corner mailbox. Before going back, she stopped at her own house. There was chocolate syrup in the refrigerator and plenty of ice cream in the freezer. She poured milk into the blender, added the syrup and ice cream, and produced two tall milkshakes that looked very professional when she added Linda's bright-colored straws.

Mr. Jameson was dozing when she returned. "Took you long enough," he said. "What's that you have there?"

Caroline handed him one of the glasses.

"Chocolate milkshakes," she said. "I made them."

He looked at her and then at the glass, while she waited expectantly, wondering what he would criticize this time.

"I'd rather have strawberry myself," he said after a minute. But he smiled — a small smile, quickly banished — and drank every drop, making loud noises with the straw when he reached the bottom of the glass.

Chapter 10

"I promised I wouldn't tell anyone." Caroline nibbled a fingernail and peered across the street through rapidly fading twilight. She and Joe were sitting on the front steps after dinner. "Mr. Jameson has lots of money in his dresser drawer, Joe. Lots of it! Even hundred-dollar bills!"

"Pretty stupid," Joe commented. He lay back, stretched his long legs, and yawned. The five-thirty call to Boston had been reassuring, and he was ready to relax. "I think Linda sounded a little stronger," he said, following his own thoughts. "And your mother was definitely cheerful. I can always tell when she's putting on an act for us and when she means it."

"So can I," Caroline said. But she wasn't as certain that things were better. Joe had sounded really lonely at the beginning of the phone call, and so her mother and Linda would naturally try to cheer him up. "About Mr. Jameson," she said. "Do you think you could take him to the bank sometime? If he'll go, that is."

Joe yawned again. "Sure, if he'll go. But he's pretty set in his ways, Carrie. I don't think he'll do it just because you and I think he should." He straightened suddenly. "What in heck is that?"

Caroline looked where he was pointing. A figure stood motionless at the corner of the yard. It was Lillina, barefoot and wearing some kind of short white robe. Her head was thrown back, and she looked at the moon with a rapt expression.

"Hi," Caroline called sharply, hoping to stop another chant to the moon goddess before it started. "This is my friend Lillina MacGregor," she explained to Joe, who watched Lillina's gliding approach with disbelief. "You know, the girl who's staying with the Restons."

Up close, Lillina's tunic appeared to be made of two not-very-long bath towels stitched together and belted with white cord. Caroline thought it looked great. She could imagine what Joe thought of it.

"This is my stepfather," she said. Joe started to get up, then sank back on the step and waved a hand at Lillina. "Nice to meet you," he said. "You — are you having a good time in Grand River?"

"Simply marvelous," Lillina drawled. But she looked uneasy. Caroline remembered what she'd said about Mr. Jameson. *I might make him uncomfortable.* . . . Lillina looked uncomfortable herself, under Joe's intense gaze. "It's very different from home, of course."

"Home is New York City, right?"

"Yes." Lillina half turned away from them, and Caroline was afraid for a moment that she was going to spin over the lawn in one of her impromptu ballets. "I really should go along home," she murmured. "I told Aunt Louise I was just going to walk over for a breath of air." She turned back to Joe, briefly. "Delightful to meet you, Mr. Cabot."

"Same here," Joe replied. "Enjoy your walk."

Caroline didn't want to hear what Joe would say when Lillina was gone. "Is it okay if I walk back to the Restons' with her?" she asked. "It's only a block."

"Guess so." Joe looked at her and then back at Lillina, as if he was having a hard time imagining them as friends. "It's okay, but you come right back. I'll stay out here and wait for you."

The sidewalk was a winding river of silver in the moonlight. Walking next to Lillina,

Caroline felt a rush of affection for her friend, and remorse at believing she might have taken the green bracelet. It could have been a shiny candy wrapper in the camera case — or nothing at all. Lillina was different from anyone else in Grand River, and that was the trouble. Joe thought she was peculiar; he hadn't bothered to hide it. *And I probably wouldn't have suspected she took the bracelet if she wasn't different from everyone else I know.* It was unfair but true.

"What did you do today, Lillina?" She wanted to make up for doubts, show that they were friends, no matter what Joe or anyone else thought.

"I worked on my novel," Lillina said dreamily. "It's going beautifully. And I made some portrait shots of Uncle Charles. I thought he was feeling a little left out, so I offered and he was very pleased." Away from Joe, her confidence seemed to have returned. She walked slowly, pointing her bare toes like a dancer. "What did you do, dear?"

"Worked for Mr. Jameson." Caroline remembered some news to share. "Guess what — I made him smile!"

Lillina laughed softly. "That's nice," she said, and sounded as if she meant it. "You could have been Eleanor, saying that. She's good with people, and so are you."

Good with people. Caroline hoped it was

true. The words made her feel almost grown-up. *Hang from a hook above your head,* she reminded herself. *Tuck in your chin.* She felt taller and slimmer, too.

They were only four houses from the Restons' bungalow when the dog appeared. At first it was just a darker blob on a dark patch of lawn, but as they came closer the blob grew and a growl issued from it. Caroline grabbed Lillina's elbow.

"That's the Kramers' German shepherd, Rafe," she whispered. "He's supposed to be locked up. He's — he's dangerous!" She was remembering the afternoon one of the Kramer boys had left the dog-run unlatched and Rafe had attacked the postman when he came up the walk. The whole neighborhood had been up in arms, and the police had warned the Kramers that the dog must be kept penned all the time. Now he was free again, and obviously in a bad mood.

"Back up, Lillina," Caroline quavered. "Let's get out of here."

Lillina shook off her hand. "Poor baby, he's just frightened," she murmured. "I can handle him, Caroline. I can handle anything." To Caroline's horror, she stepped forward and held out her fingers. "I'll just let him know we're friends."

"No!" Caroline's protest was a terrified squeak. "He's mean, Lillina! He bites!

Please!" The hulking figure of the dog was like a nightmare come to life.

"Animals like me," Lillina said confidently. "They know I understand them. Good doggy. Good Rafe."

Good Rafe snarled deep in his throat. He braced himself to leap, a posture so threatening that there was no mistaking what he intended to do if she came a step closer.

"Well!" Lillina sounded annoyed rather than frightened. "He's not very bright, is he? I mean, I've never had the slightest trouble — "

Caroline was halfway across the road. "Come *on*," she urged. "If we get away from his yard, maybe he'll forget about us."

Lillina gave up. She backed across the road, while the dog continued to snarl. They made their way along the sidewalk, not speaking, until they were directly opposite the Restons' house. Then they dashed across the road. Caroline was ahead, but Lillina caught up quickly, her long legs a blur in the dark.

"What in the world!" Mrs. Reston struggled to her feet as they burst without warning through the front door. Darning thread, scissors, and socks spilled across the carpet. "Charles!" she shrieked. "Charles, come here!"

Mr. Reston hurried in from the kitchen as the girls tumbled onto the sofa, gasping for breath. He was wearing pajamas and a bathrobe and carrying a coffee mug. When he saw Caroline, he looked embarrassed.

Lillina pushed her hair back from her face. "It's nothing, really," she gasped. "Just a silly little fright — "

Nothing! "Kramers' dog is loose," Caroline said. "He snarled at us, and he would have jumped us if we hadn't backed across the road. It was awful!"

Mrs. Reston rushed to the door, kicking balled-up socks in every direction. She peered out into the night. "Charles, they could have been killed!" she exclaimed. "That animal is a monster! What are you going to do?"

"Is he out there now?" Mr. Reston sounded as if he hoped the answer would be no.

"He's not sitting outside the front door waiting for you, if that's what you mean. He's *lurking* somewhere, and so no one is safe, and — "

"I'll call Tom Kramer," Mr. Reston said. "He'll take care of it."

"He'd better," said Mrs. Reston. Her cheeks were pink with outrage. "You tell him he could be sued for thousands of dollars if that dog had touched the girls. You tell him you're going to call the police. Tell him — "

"I'll take care of it." Mr. Reston escaped to the kitchen. His round baby face, pale blue robe, and floppy slippers didn't suggest a knight-to-the-rescue, but he sounded determined. With Mrs. Reston shouting instructions, it would have been hard to be otherwise.

"Now you girls just relax," Mrs. Reston said. "Charles will take care of everything. He's marvelous in an emergency." She stopped to listen for a moment to the gentle murmur of her husband's voice on the kitchen telephone. "What I think we should do is have a nice cup of hot chocolate. To calm you down."

"My stepfather's waiting for me," Caroline said. "I'm supposed to come right back."

"Well, he'll understand if you call him," Mrs. Reston said comfortably. "You'll have to give Tom Kramer time to pen up that beast before you start home."

Caroline nodded. She was in no hurry to face Barker Road alone. While she called Joe to tell him what had happened, Mrs. Reston bustled around making cocoa and filling a plate with cookies.

"I told Tom he'd better get a new lock for his dog-run," Mr. Reston announced when they were settled around the kitchen table. "I told him he'd better start checking for himself to make sure the gate is fastened. You can't trust those boys to do it." He sounded pleased with the way he'd coped.

Lillina perched on her chair between the Restons like a rare red-crested bird. She'd been unusually silent for the last few minutes, but now she spoke. "We shouldn't have let him scare us away," she said, apparently still annoyed at her failure to charm Rafe. "Some neighbors of ours had a beautiful dog — a Doberman — but it had been badly treated when it was a puppy, and it snapped at people all the time. I was absolutely the only person outside of their family who could get near it. From the very first — "

Mrs. Reston cut this reminiscence short. "Trying to make friends with a snarling dog is ridiculous," she said flatly. "You could have been badly hurt."

No one said anything for a moment. Caroline agreed wholeheartedly with Mrs. Reston, but she didn't want to say so. "Lillina told me about the portraits she's doing of you," she said, to change the subject. "I bet they'll be very good."

Mr. Reston looked puzzled for a moment, and then his expression cleared. "Oh, yes. It's nice to have pictures. She'll want reminders of her visit, I guess."

"*Lillian* takes lots of snaps," Mrs. Reston emphasized the name. "It's a nice hobby."

Lillina nibbled an oatmeal cookie and didn't bother to protest that photography was more than a hobby to her. *The Restons don't understand her at all*, Caroline thought. It was easy to believe there might be many "misunderstandings" this summer.

The telephone rang just as they finished their cocoa. It was Mr. Kramer, saying that Rafe was back in his pen. Then Mrs. Reston insisted on calling Joe so he could meet Caroline halfway home. "I'd never forgive myself if something happened," she boomed. "Lillian is a great one for walking in the evening, and I don't approve, I'm sure. Anything could happen. . . ."

How strange it was to hear Lillina talked about as if she were a little girl! The odd thing was that she actually looked younger, sitting between the Restons in the small, shining kitchen. The white tunic looked different here too. It *was* just two bath towels sewn together, and rather clumsily sewn at that.

"Thanks for the cocoa," Caroline said. "I'll see you, Lillina."

Lillina looked up from her cocoa and smiled. "That will be wonderful, dear," she said. "Maybe we'll have another adventure."

But not with a killer dog. Caroline was uneasy; it was the way she'd felt at the mall. Lillina was an unpredictable, firecracker kind of person, always rocketing off in unexpected directions. *Firecrackers can be scary,* she thought as she hurried along the sidewalk toward home.

The moon was brilliant now, and she could see Joe waiting at the curve, his tall, broad-shouldered figure unmistakable. "Thanks for coming," she said, when they met. She felt like throwing her arms around him, but she didn't. "I'll never forget that darned dog snarling at us in the dark."

"I'll bet your nutty friend attracts trouble the way honey attracts flies," Joe said in reply. They turned toward home, and that was his only comment on his meeting with Lillina.

It was enough.

Chapter 11

During the two weeks that followed, Caroline saw Lillina only briefly. Mrs. Reston refused to permit any more evening walks, and Caroline usually had chores to do in the afternoon when she returned from Mr. Jameson's house. She and Lillina did plan a picnic one day, but Lillina canceled it at the last minute because of another "tiny misunderstanding."

"We'll get together soon," she promised on the telephone. "Tell me about your job, Caroline. I want to write to Eleanor about it."

Caroline didn't know if her job was going well or not. She was still working, but Mr. Jameson continued to complain, and sometimes he shouted at her. He didn't use the walker that she always left within his reach. He refused Joe's offer to take him downtown "if you have any errands there."

He never complimented Caroline on the lunches she prepared for him, even though she was becoming more daring with her menus. She made French toast at home for Joe, and then made it again the next day for Mr. Jameson. She fixed waffles for breakfast, and when Joe pronounced them "not bad at all," she carried the waffle iron across the street to Mr. Jameson's kitchen. She tried her mother's recipe for tuna-burgers, combining tuna, onions, hard-boiled eggs, and mushroom soup. "Gettin' pretty fancy," was all Mr. Jameson said after he'd cleaned his plate.

Still, she had a feeling that he waited eagerly for her arrival each morning. One day, they sorted through a box of letters and clippings he'd been saving for years. She saw pictures of a round, smiling Mrs. Jameson who had died long ago. She learned that Mr. Jameson had won an amateur swimming championship when he was twenty-six and had been the Grand River bowling champion when he was forty. She found out that he'd once worked on an oil rig in the Gulf of Mexico and for years had driven a semitrailer truck all over the United States. After the box was back on the closet shelf, Caroline wondered if he'd suggested the "sorting" to show her, and himself, that he hadn't always been a sick old man.

A letter came from his niece Jean, and Mr.

Jameson gave it to Caroline to read. It was full of news about Jean's family and questions about her uncle's health. "Please ask that nice neighbor of yours to write again and tell me more about yourself," it said. "I worry."

"How many hours have you been here?" Mr. Jameson asked abruptly at the end of the second week. He was in his usual chair in front of the television set. "Turn that stupid thing off."

Caroline obeyed. "It's been about two weeks," she said. "Every day except one."

"That ain't what I asked you," Mr. Jameson snapped. "How many hours?"

"I — I don't know."

He rolled his eyes in disgust. "Never goin' to get anywhere that way," he said. "It's twenty hours and a half, total. I kept track in my head. Good thing somebody did. Is two-fifty an hour okay with you?"

Without waiting for an answer, he struggled to his feet and lurched toward the little hall leading to his bedroom. Caroline followed him into the bedroom and opened the top dresser drawer when he had trouble doing it himself. He pushed the box of stationery out of the way and stood looking at the money underneath. After a moment, he took out two bills and laid them on the dresser. Then he put the box back in place, and Caroline closed the drawer.

"Those are yours," he said gruffly. "You get a quarter besides. Take it out of the can in the kitchen." He scowled. "What's the matter? You expectin' more?"

"Oh, no!" Caroline stared at the fifty-dollar bill and the one, lying side by side. "That's plenty!"

Mr. Jameson sniffed and began his uncertain journey back to the living room. "It's what you earned," he snapped, "so that's what you get."

Caroline crumpled the money in her fist. She felt like a millionaire! If Linda were home, she'd run across the street this very minute to show her the money. If only *somebody* were there!

"I'm going to England for Christmas," she told Mr. Jameson, her excitement bubbling over. For the first time the trip seemed possible. Just two or three more weeks on the job . . .

"You ain't goin' on what you earn from me," Mr. Jameson said. "Don't you know how much an airplane ticket costs?"

Caroline explained about Jeannie Richmond's invitation and Grandma Parks's offer to pay for the flight. "All I have to earn is my spending money," she said.

"Your folks goin' to let a little thing like you go off by herself?"

"I'm not so little." Caroline wished she hadn't started this conversation. "I'd better fix your lunch now. It's after twelve."

She was glad she'd brought him a special treat, since it had turned out to be a special day. "I made soup last night," she announced when his tray was ready. "There was a recipe in the paper. I hope you like it."

Mr. Jameson's scowl deepened. "Too hot for soup," he said. "Don't you know that?"

Caroline set the tray in front of him. "It's cold soup," she said triumphantly. "It's cucumber soup."

Mr. Jameson made a face. "Never heard of it," he said. "I like my cucumbers in a salad." He dipped a spoon into the pale green soup and lifted it to his lips, while Caroline watched and fingered the fifty-one dollars in her pocket.

"Tastes queer," he announced. "What'd you put in it besides cucumbers?"

"Buttermilk," Caroline told him. "Green onions and parsley. My stepfather liked it."

"Your stepfather and I would probably disagree about a lot of things." Mr. Jameson pushed the soup bowl away. "I'll have a peanut-butter sandwich," he said. "If that ain't too ordinary for a high-class cook."

Any other day, Caroline's feelings would have been hurt, but today she was too happy to care. She made the sandwich hurriedly, and a half hour later with Mr. Jameson stretched out for his nap, she was back across the street. Lillina waited on the front steps of the Cabots' house. When she saw Caroline coming, she strolled to meet her with her elegant high-fashion walk.

"I had to come," she murmured. "This has been the most heavenly day!"

"What happened?" Caroline had been about to display her fifty-one dollars, but she stopped.

"Well, first of all," Lillina said, whirling Miss America style up the walk to the house, "first of all, I've practically finished my novel. And it really is excellent, Caroline, though I probably shouldn't say so."

"That's terrific!" Caroline exclaimed. She was genuinely pleased, even though finishing a novel made her fifty-one dollars seem less thrilling.

"And," Lillina rushed on, "I had a marvelous letter from dear Frederick. Our house is coming along beautifully, and guess what! He's bought me a puppy!"

"A puppy!" No wonder Lillina was excited. Her eyes were almost feverishly bright, and her cheeks were pink under their sprinkle of freckles. "What kind of puppy?"

"An Afghan hound." Lillina took a folded piece of paper from the pocket of her lavender skirt and spread it on the step between them. It was a photograph of a model posed at the top of a flight of stone steps. She had long hair, parted in the middle and falling straight on either side of her thin face. The dog beside her had a thin face, too, and its long hair fell to its shoulders. "That's an Afghan," Lillina said. "Won't it be marvelous to take her for walks in Central Park?" She leaned back on her elbows and smiled down at the picture, as if the puppy itself were sitting there at her side.

"I get along with all animals," she said. Caroline knew she was thinking about Rafe. "I can hardly wait to see my puppy."

Caroline felt a twinge of envy and was ashamed. After all, Lillina was her friend. "I thought it was dangerous to walk in Central Park," she said.

"Not with an Afghan," Lillina retorted. "And I have something else to tell you, Caroline. Or rather, something to give you — a surprise. Let's go to the Talbott Inn for ice cream, to celebrate. Then I'll give you your surprise."

"The Talbott Inn is expensive," Caroline said, but she was ready to go. After all, Lillina didn't know it yet, but Caroline had something to celebrate, too. And she had two dollar bills and some change in her piggy bank. She could order the biggest banana split on the menu without dipping into her brand-new travel fund.

Forty-five minutes later, Lillina was leading the way across the lobby of the Inn. It was a beautiful room, all gold and green and brown, with a huge metal urn full of dried flowers on a pedestal in the center of the carpet. Caroline looked around admiringly, but Lillina seemed to take all this grandeur for granted. She stopped first at the entrance to the formal dining room and stood in the archway looking around with an air of haughty approval. A piano tinkled softly in one corner.

"We must have dinner here one evening," Lillina said. "It's rather nice, isn't it?" Then she led the way back across the lobby to the coffee shop.

"Now," she said, after they were seated in a sunny yellow booth and had ordered their banana splits. "Here's your surprise, Caroline. It came in the same mail as my letter from Frederick." She produced a pale gray envelope addressed to Miss Caroline Cabot, in care of Mrs. Frederick MacGregor, 801 Barker Road, Grand River, Wisconsin.

"I'm sorry the envelope is damaged," Lillina said. "Uncle Charles collects stamps, and this was a new one he especially wanted. I told him you wouldn't mind."

"Who's it from?" Caroline asked. But she knew. The letter was from Eleanor. Eleanor, who looked like Caroline and carried herself proudly, who had a glamorous, talented sister but didn't let it bother her, because her own life was full of interesting projects. Eleanor, who was thinking of becoming a nurse someday because she was good with people. Eleanor, who would understand how thrilling it was to receive fifty-one dollars for sticking with a difficult job. Caroline slid the single sheet of gray stationery from its envelope and read the typewritten message:

Dear Caroline,

My sister Lillina has told me all about you. She says you and she have marvelous times together. She says you are a very good friend, and I'm sure that if I were in Grand River, we'd be good friends, too. So I thought I'd write and say hello.

I hope your job is going all right. Lillina says the person you work for is very cross, but you help him a lot. That's really great.

I'm sorry your sister is sick. She must be a wonderful person, but I think you must be wonderful, too.

Last week I had my hair cut short, and I like it this way very much. Lillina says you and I look a lot alike, so I thought maybe you'd want to have your hair cut the same way. I'm sending a picture I found in a magazine. This is the way my hair looks now.

If you want to write to me, we can be pen pals. Good-bye for now.

*Your friend,
Eleanor*

Caroline read the letter twice before passing it across the table. "You can read it if you want to," she said. "Eleanor and I are going to be pen pals." She examined the picture. The girl in the photo was dark-haired and a little older than Caroline. Her hair was short and shining; it turned up slightly at the ends, and there was a suggestion of soft bangs across her forehead. Caroline held up the picture for Lillina to see.

"Marvelous," Lillina said. "That's the absolutely perfect style for Eleanor. She hates spending a lot of time on her looks, but this cut will be easy to take care of."

Caroline touched her bushy ponytail. It was fastened with a rubber band at the nape of her neck.

"I *could* have mine cut, I guess," she said slowly. "I don't like fussing with it, that's for sure." She studied the picture again.

Lillina shrugged. "It's up to you, dear. I enjoy arranging my hair — but then, we're very different, aren't we? And if this cut is right for Eleanor — "

" — then it's right for me," Caroline finished. She could hardly wait to do it. She would tell Eleanor when she answered the letter.

The thought of the haircut — of being like Eleanor in yet another way — made the triple-dip, strawberry and hot fudge banana split an anticlimax when it finally arrived. Caroline read the letter two more times while she was eating.

"I can lend you money for the haircut," Lillina offered. "If it's a problem, I mean."

That reminded Caroline of her own good news. "I was paid today." She tried to match Lillina's casual tone. "So I have money. I have half of what I need to go to England."

Lillina threw up her hands in a dramatic gesture of amazement. "That's marvelous!" she exclaimed. "I'm really proud of you, Caroline."

Caroline felt a little shiver of concern. She was pretty sure her mother and Joe had forgotten all about the Richmonds' invitation. What if they said no! For the first time she realized she didn't want the sheltering, smothering kind of love that they showered on Linda.

When the bill arrived, Lillina picked it up. "My treat, Caroline," she said grandly. "Because my novel is nearly finished, and our house is nearly ready, and because I have a puppy — and because you're going to England, of course." She took a wallet from her floppy shoulder bag and produced a thick wad of bills. "Actually, this is Frederick's treat," she said. "He always sends much more money than I need."

Caroline protested, but not much. She would pay next time, she promised herself — after the money for the trip to England was in the bank. *And after Mom and Joe say I can go.*

She followed Lillina out of the coffee shop, walking tall and holding Eleanor's letter as if it were a good-luck charm she would keep forever.

Chapter 12

"You should have told me," Joe said. "You should have checked with your mother before you did a thing like that."

"Don't you like it?" Caroline touched the back of her neck, which felt strangely bare.

Joe shook his head impatiently. "That's not the point, and you know it, Carrie. Cutting your hair is a big step."

"Well, if I asked, you'd say 'Do what you want.' And Mom isn't here, so I couldn't ask her, could I?"

"Watch your tone," Joe snapped. "You could have called the clinic and talked it over. I suppose your weird friend convinced you you should do it."

"Nobody *convinced* me." Caroline scooped up her dust cloth and the bottle of lemon oil and started out of the living room. "And I'm sorry I bothered to polish all the furniture if nobody's even going to notice. I can't do anything right around here."

"Now just wait a minute!" Joe caught her arm and swung her around. "You don't look like yourself, Carrie. You don't even walk the way you used to. Give me a chance to get accustomed to it. What's more, you don't sound like yourself either, and I don't want to get used to *that*. What in blazes has happened to you?"

Caroline didn't know what had happened to her. She'd felt different ever since she'd come home from the beauty salon. It was as if the hair stylist had snipped away a Caroline-cocoon and sent a sleek new butterfly-person out into the world. A person who refused to be ignored or taken for granted!

"I just want you to care what I do," she said, close to tears. "I don't just want to *be* here, I want to be somebody."

Joe released her arm, and they stared at each other. Caroline wondered where those words had come from; she hadn't meant to say them, didn't even remember thinking them before they spouted from her lips.

"Of course you're somebody." Now Joe sounded confused. "What the heck kind of talk is that?" He slumped into a chair and rubbed his forehead in mock despair. "Girls!" he muttered. "I wish your mother was home."

"So do I." Caroline stood uncertainly in

front of him. She had never challenged Joe before, had always tried to please him. She still wanted to please him. What was going on here, anyway?

Abruptly, Joe grinned and raised his hands in defeat. "Your hair looks good," he said. "I like it short. I admit it."

"Thanks."

"But you could have told me in advance that you wanted to do it, right?"

"Right."

He leaned back, watching her closely. "So what's the big fuss, right?"

"Right." Caroline returned the smile, much relieved. But as she carried the furniture polish and the dust cloth to the back-hall cupboard, she knew that neither she nor Joe would forget this conversation. It had burst upon them like a small tornado and had left them both surprised and upset.

In her bedroom, Caroline studied herself in the mirror. It had taken four days to get enough nerve to call the beauty salon, and six more days to get an appointment. In that time she'd changed her mind about the haircut a half-dozen times. During three calls to her mother and Linda she had clamped her lips on the subject, because if she did this she wanted it to be her own decision.

As soon as the appointment was set, she'd written to Eleanor and given the letter to

Lillina to send with her own. The reply had come immediately, this time enclosed with a letter to Lillina from her mother. Caroline kept the pale gray sheet open on her dresser where she could look at it often. *I hope you'll like your haircut as much as I like mine. I wish I could see the miniatures you make. My sister says you are very talented.*

The telephone rang and Joe answered, sounding subdued. It wasn't her mother calling; his tone was usually lighter when a call came from Boston. Caroline picked up the tiny rocker she'd assembled the night before and tested each part to make sure the glue was holding. She would paint it a soft blue-gray, she decided.

"Carrie! Telephone."

She put the rocker on the card table and hurried down the hall. "It's Mrs. Reston," Joe said, cocking an eyebrow at her. "She wants to know if you'd like to go to church with them tomorrow."

"To church?" Caroline picked up the phone and listened while the invitation was repeated. "Unless you're going to your own church, of course," Mrs. Reston said. "I wouldn't want to interfere."

"No," Caroline said. "That's okay." She couldn't remember the last time she'd gone to church. Her parents never wanted to leave

Linda alone on Sunday mornings, and Caroline didn't like to go by herself.

"That's fine then, dear," Mrs. Reston said. "Lillian will be very pleased, I'm sure. I'd call her to the phone, but she's in her room working and I don't like to interrupt."

She must be going over the novel one more time, Caroline thought. Joe would have to stop talking about "your weird friend" when Lillina MacGregor's name was on the bestseller list and she was interviewed on the *Today* show in New York.

She would be glad to see Lillina again and show off her haircut. Since the celebration at the Talbott Inn, they'd had only one afternoon together. Lying on a blanket in Caroline's hideaway behind the toolshed, Lillina had alternated between bursts of excitement and long periods of quiet. She'd talked about her novel, about the new photographs she was taking, and about the modeling career that awaited her in New York. She'd described the way she was going to decorate her new house, and Caroline was pleased that one of the bedrooms was going to look very much like Linda's. But then, without warning, the sparkle had faded from the slanted brown eyes and the thin face had become strained and remote. *She's probably working so hard, she's all tired out.* Caroline could picture her friend sitting up most of the night, reading her manuscript and making last-minute changes.

"I didn't know your redheaded buddy was a big churchgoer," Joe said that evening over Caroline's latest experiment, pork chops topped with packaged dressing and celery soup. His expression was solemn, his voice teasing.

"I don't know if she is or not," Caroline retorted. "We never talked about it. But I'm glad they asked me to go along." She missed church. And she had a lot of people to pray for. There was Linda, first of all, and her mother and Joe. There was Mr. Jameson, who was becoming more shaky and more unhappy each day. And she wanted to say thank you for good friends like Lillina. She could pray at home, of course, but she looked forward to the service, with lots of people around her, all of them thinking of those who mattered to them most.

The next morning she waited on the front steps until the Restons' dark green Olds came around the curve and made a U-turn in front of the house. To Caroline's surprise, Mr. Reston was alone in the front seat and Lillina in back.

"My wife sends her regrets," Mr. Reston said as Caroline climbed in beside Lillina.

"She woke up feeling ill this morning and decided to rest."

Lillina looked as if she should have stayed in bed, too. Her eyes were bloodshot, and she was very pale. She smiled wanly and said, "I love your hair, dear." For the rest of the trip she stared out the window, leaving Caroline to discuss the weather with Mr. Reston.

The church was a small white building with a steeple, on the outskirts of town. In winter, with a carpet of snow around it, it would look like a Christmas card, but now the country road was lined with cars, and clusters of people stood on the lawn, chatting and enjoying the sun. A bulletin board announced a special guest speaker for the morning service: Dwight Lloyd Boynton. Caroline said the name over to herself, liking the sound of it.

Inside, folding chairs had been set up along the center aisle and in the space behind the pews. Mr. Reston gestured toward a pew near the back, but Lillina didn't seem to notice. She glided toward the front in her white blouse and white linen skirt, and Caroline and Mr. Reston trotted obediently behind her.

As soon as they were seated, Caroline took a pencil from a little rack fastened to the back of the pew ahead and wrote Lillina a note on an envelope meant for an offering. "Don't you like my hair?" She underlined "like" three times.

Lillina took the pencil and scribbled a reply. "I think it's marvelous." She underlined "marvelous" four times, then added, "Had a headache this morning. Better now. Tiny misunderstanding with Aunt Louise. Something unusual is going to happen today — can you feel it?" She underlined "unusual" five times.

"I just feel hot," Caroline wrote back. But she was much relieved. She had felt kind of, well, pretty, this morning, and Lillina's indifference had been a dash of cold water to her spirits.

The church was not at all like the big stone building where Caroline had been baptized and where she'd gone to Sunday school until she was nine. There were no candles, no stained glass, no carpeting on the floor. Sun blazed through the clear windows and a ceiling fan whirled noisily overhead. An upright piano stood against one wall, and two straight-backed chairs waited behind the simple altar. But in spite of the plainness, or perhaps because of it, Caroline felt comfortable here. She was very glad she'd accepted the Restons' invitation.

The little auditorium filled quickly. Soon a heavy blond woman entered through a side door and sat down at the piano. She stretched her fingers over the keys and began to play. Caroline recognized the melody — an old hymn she'd always enjoyed — but she'd never heard it played this way before. The pudgy hands raced up and down the keyboard, letting the tune find its way through a cascade of tinkling notes. When the hymn ended, another one, just as familiar, began. Caroline was so entranced that she didn't notice when the minister and the guest speaker came in and sat down in the chairs behind the altar.

Lillina's sharp elbow dug into her ribs. "He's handsome!" she whispered. "Look!"

She was staring at the guest speaker, not at the minister, whose thin red face was beaded with sweat above his heavy robe. Dwight Lloyd Boynton didn't look hot at all. He wore a white suit and a deep blue tie. His blond hair fell in waves nearly to his shoulders, and he had pale blue eyes framed by thick lashes. He looked about eighteen.

"He's like an angel," Lillina whispered.

Caroline agreed, though she thought it was a little disloyal of Lillina even to notice another man's appearance when she had a wonderful husband of her own.

The minister led an opening prayer and then read a long passage from the Bible. Caroline prayed hard for the people on her mental list. The pianist began another hymn, played in the same rippling style, and the congregation sang vigorously. Then the guest speaker moved to the pulpit.

"Good morning, sinners." Dwight Lloyd Boynton had a kindly, almost teasing smile that took most of the sting from his greeting. "I've come with good news for every one of you."

Caroline listened intently. She didn't like being called a sinner, but as he talked she began to feel that he was speaking directly to her. Everybody made mistakes, he said. Everyone got mixed up about what God wanted him or her to do. The good news was that it was never too late to change. You could envy your beautiful sister, and God would help you to stop. You could be angry with your parents, and if you really wanted God's help, you had it. You could feel invisible, and God would help you become a real person. Dwight Lloyd Boynton didn't give those particular examples, but Caroline knew what kinds of sins he was talking about.

"Be joyous!" he commanded. Caroline felt her heart lift. She could change; she had already changed a lot. It had been weeks since she'd had to look into a mirror to make sure she was really there.

But when the speaker invited the congregation to come to the altar to receive his special blessing, Caroline shrank back in the pew. She was joyous, but it was a private feeling; she didn't want to get up in front of all those people. If Eleanor were here, she probably wouldn't do it either. They were people who kept their big, important feelings to themselves. God would have to understand that, the way He understood everything else.

There was a stirring at her side, and Lillina stood up. She looked as if she were in a trance.

"I'm going," she whispered. She brushed past Caroline and stepped into the aisle.

Caroline glanced at Mr. Reston. There was a smile on his round face, and he was watching Lillina proudly. Maybe that was why they were in church this morning, Caroline thought suddenly. Maybe Mr. and Mrs. Reston worried about Lillina because she was so different from the people who lived in Grand River, and they hoped that going to church with them would make her more like other girls they knew.

If that was it, Caroline decided, they were going to be disappointed. Lillina glowed like a slim white candle among the people clustered at the altar. She was taller than the women and most of the men, and she stood with her head thrown back dramatically, so the gleaming red hair fell nearly to her waist. Dwight Lloyd Boynton went from one person to another, putting his hand on each head and murmuring a blessing, but he kept glancing, uneasily, at Lillina. Finally she was the only person left at the altar; the others had received their blessing and returned to their pews. He put out a cautious hand toward Lillina, as if he wondered what might happen next. Caroline held her breath.

When his hand touched her head, Lillina dropped gracefully to her knees, startling him and everyone in the congregation. She knelt there like a statue, until Dwight Lloyd Boynton grasped her folded hands and lifted her to her feet. "Go with the Lord's blessing," he said, and cleared his throat. Someone giggled. People moved restlessly in their seats.

White skirt flaring around her, Lillina turned to the congregation and smiled radiantly. Caroline's face burned. She tried to hang on to her happy feelings (*Be joyous!*), but a wave of irritation threatened to spoil everything. Why did Lillina have to put on her Miss America act here? Why make a dramatic scene in church?

The minister stood up to pray once more, and there was a final hymn while the offering plate was passed. Then the congregation filed from the church. A fresh breeze lifted Caroline's new bangs as she stepped outside, but she was too annoyed to enjoy it. She stood stonily at Lillina's side, while Mr. Reston greeted friends and stopped to chat with the minister.

"How could you do that?" she demanded finally. "It was so *corny*, Lillina!"

Lillina looked at her in astonishment. "Do what? I've been blessed, Caroline. I've been forgiven for my sins."

"Well, you didn't have to put on a show," Caroline snapped. "You wanted to impress Dwight Lloyd Boynton, that's all. You shouldn't *act* in church."

Lillina looked genuinely hurt. "I don't know what you mean," she said. "I just did what felt right. I mean, I've made mistakes like everyone else, and I wanted to be forgiven, and now I am."

Caroline took a deep breath. "You weren't just acting? You really weren't?"

"Of course not." Lillina put a hand over her heart and looked ready to get down on her knees again. "It was a marvelous feeling, Caroline. I feel so much better now. You should have gone to the altar, too." She paused, and took Caroline's silence as an apology. "I forgive you, dear," she said gently. "You just didn't understand."

It was true. Caroline realized she didn't understand Lillina any better than the Restons did. She was — different. But it was impossible to stay angry with her for very long. When Mr. Reston bustled up and said wasn't it a fine service, Caroline said yes, it was. She was glad he would have a good report to take home to Mrs. Reston. And she would be joyous herself, a better person, too, with God's help. Dwight Lloyd Boynton had given her a lot to think about.

"I would have gone to the altar even if he wasn't handsome," Lillina whispered on the way home. "Actually, I much prefer distinguished-looking older men, like Frederick."

Caroline was glad to hear it. It was several days later before she began to guess what, exactly, the mistakes were for which Lillina wanted forgiveness.

Chapter 13

"Want to take in a movie tonight, Carrie? You ought to show off the new haircut." They were in the kitchen having breakfast.

Ever since their talk Saturday morning, Joe had been treating Caroline as if she were a Delicate Person. Almost the way he treated Linda! He smiled each time their eyes met, and he made conversation at breakfast and dinner, even when he was tired and she knew he would rather be quiet.

"Sure," she said, enjoying the pampering. "We can eat early."

"Want me to do hamburgers on the grill?"

Caroline blinked. Joe always said a charcoal fire was more trouble than it was worth. "That's okay," she said. "I'll fry them on the stove — and I'll fix some baked beans."

Joe took a last sip from his coffee mug and pushed back his chair. "You'll be over at Jameson's today, huh?"

She nodded. Not only was she going to help Mr. Jameson; she intended to make him smile again. She was sure she could do more to make his life pleasant, and she had promised God and Dwight Lloyd Boynton that she was going to do it.

When she opened Mr. Jameson's front door later that morning, the house was so quiet that she entered on tiptoe. Usually the television set was on, but today the only sound was the tick-tick of the clock next to the front door.

"Mr. Jameson?" Her voice sounded very loud.

"In here."

She ran down the hall to the bedroom. Mr. Jameson lay face down on the floor between the bed and the dresser. When she knelt beside him, he struck the floor with a bony fist. "Get me up!" he commanded. "Make yourself useful, girl."

Caroline took a shaky breath and considered what seemed like an impossible order. Mr. Jameson was thin, but he was tall and big-boned. She planted a foot on either side of his chest and grasped his shoulders. Without much hope, she tried to lift him.

"Not like that," the old man snarled. "You ain't goin' to be able to do it by yourself. Tell me when you're ready to lift, and I'll help."

She got in position for another try. Mr.

Jameson rocked back and forth until his arms were under him.

"Now!" She gave a mighty tug. Mr. Jameson managed a one-sided pushup that lifted him off the floor and tipped him over on his side.

"It's no use," Caroline gasped. "I'll go out and find somebody to help us. Maybe Mrs. Kramer — "

"NO!" His face turned a deep red, and he thumped the floor again. "I don't want any busybodies in here mindin' my business. Why are you such a quitter?"

"I wasn't quitting!" Caroline exclaimed, beginning to get angry in spite of her concern. "I just don't see how — "

"I don't want anybody else," Mr. Jameson insisted. He rested one arm on the edge of the bed. "Now, when I say so, you push from behind. It'll work if you just make up your mind to do it."

Caroline bit her lip. She got behind Mr. Jameson, and when he said "Now!" she pushed up and forward with all her might. He rocked onto his knees and leaned on the bed as if he were saying his prayers.

"Again!" he roared. This time he staggered to his feet and bent over the bed, breathing heavily. Caroline ran into the living room to get the walker. When she returned, he was sitting on the bed.

"What's that for?" he demanded. "Take it away."

"But that's why you fell down," Caroline protested. "You need the walker. Doesn't the visiting nurse tell you to use it?"

Mr. Jameson snorted. "I use it when she's here — darn fool makes such a fuss, I have to. But I don't have to now!"

"You should." Caroline forced herself to meet the old man's glare. He looked ready to explode.

"You go home," he growled. "I don't want any more help today. You done enough."

Caroline stared at him. "But your lunch," she protested. "And you said we were going to write to Jean again. . . ."

"Go on home, I tell you. Don't want any lunch. Don't feel like writin' a letter either."

It was no use. The fall had ended any chance of cheering him up today. He hated being helpless, and Caroline thought he probably hated her, too, for having seen him that way.

What could she do to help? First she would have to tell Joe what had happened. Maybe she could even write to Mr. Jameson's niece and tell her that her uncle wouldn't use his walker and was in constant danger of falling.

"Now, don't you go blabbin' about this," the old man roared, as if he'd been reading her mind. "I won't have it, you hear? Anybody can slip once 'n a while. . . ." He looked at her slyly. "You tell people about this, and they're goin' to clap me in a nursin' home so fast it'll make your head spin. Then you won't have a job anymore, and you won't go on that trip you told me about."

Caroline flinched, and Mr. Jameson looked triumphant. "Go on home now," he ordered. "Take that blasted thing" — he pointed at the walker — "take that with you."

Caroline carried the walker back to the living room. She considered making lunch, whether he wanted it or not. Better not to, she decided. He was angry, and he wasn't likely to calm down as long as she was there.

"I'll see you tomorrow," she called in a low voice and hurried out before he could tell her not to bother.

She couldn't stop thinking about what had happened. At home, while she changed the beds and did the laundry, she pictured Mr. Jameson lurching around his little house. In the late afternoon, frying bacon and chopping onion to add to the baked beans, she kept seeing him on the floor of his bedroom. What if he'd struck his head when he fell? What if she hadn't gone to work today and he'd had to lie there until the housekeeper came to make his evening meal?

When the beans were in the oven, she went to her bedroom. The blue rocker looked just right in the new little family room. The walls of the room were covered with a sticky-backed paper that looked like wood paneling. The woven blue rug set off the rocking chair perfectly. Caroline wound a little ball of yellow yarn and stuck a pair of toothpick needles through it. She dropped the ball on the rocker, as if the knitter had just gotten up and left it there. Opposite the chair was a pine table "borrowed" from one of the first rooms she'd constructed. There were postage-stamp-sized pictures on the walls, and the dainty lace curtains were cut from an old blouse of her mother's. A nutshell vase was filled with dainty dried flowers.

She examined the room critically, looking for something else she could do to improve it. Something to keep her busy so she didn't have to think. . . . She winced, imagining a tiny Mr. Jameson lying face down on the blue rug.

She made up her mind. Joe would have to be told about the fall. Telling was the right thing to do, and she'd promised herself to be a better person. Almost certainly, Joe would say Mr. Jameson mustn't live alone anymore. Almost certainly, he would tell the nurse who came every day, and she would make Mr. Jameson move to a nursing home.

The job would be over.

There were now seventy-five dollars in

Caroline's bank account. She'd used some of the money she'd earned to buy furniture kits and rolls of dollhouse wallpaper. With another month before school started, she'd assumed she'd have plenty of time to bring her savings up to one hundred dollars.

That's not what matters, Caroline. She pictured the words typed on Eleanor's neat gray stationery. *What matters is Mr. Jameson.*

She returned to the kitchen and took the ground beef from the refrigerator. She would tell Joe at supper, she decided. She would do the right thing, even if it meant giving up the trip to England.

The baked beans were delicious, the flavors nicely blended by an hour of slow cooking. "Just as good as your mother's," Joe said with determined enthusiasm. His glance flicked to the chair where Mrs. Cabot always sat. "Wonder what *they're* having for dinner tonight," he said. There was no need to explain whom he meant by "they."

Almost as if the look had been a signal, the telephone rang. Joe dropped his hamburger on his plate and jumped up. He was halfway down the hall to the phone before the second ring.

Caroline waited until a hearty "Hi there!" told her who it was. Then she hurried to

Linda's bedroom and picked up the white phone next to the bed.

"Mom?"

"Darlings!" Mrs. Cabot sounded excited. "Guess what! Great news — we're coming home!"

"You aren't!" Joe was afraid to believe it. "I thought you'd be there all summer. I thought — " He stopped, overwhelmed.

"That's great, Mom." The pink and white bedroom was suddenly full of Linda's presence. They would be able to talk; she'd tell Linda all about Lillina and Eleanor, about Mr. Jameson, about Dwight Lloyd Boynton — maybe even about the trip to England, now that it was no longer going to happen.

"How's Linda?" Joe demanded. "Is she really well enough to come home?"

"Well, she's better." A shadow touched Mrs. Cabot's voice, and Caroline gripped the phone so tightly her hand tingled. "A little better, anyway. Her doctor says she's gone as far as she can go with the treatment. I'm sure you'll see some improvement," she added quickly. "We're both so anxious to get back ... aren't we, dear?"

Linda's soft voice murmured in the background. For a moment they were all silent, aware of what was not being said. Caroline remembered her sister's despair at the thought of going to a hospital again. She hadn't expected the treatment to help, and it hadn't. Not much, anyway.

"... this weekend," Mrs. Cabot was saying in response to Joe's question. She would call with the flight number and arrival time later.

"We'll be waiting," Joe said. "Boy, will we be waiting!" They all laughed, relieved that a painful moment had passed. There was a flurry of good-byes.

When her mother had hung up, Caroline sat on the edge of the bed and tried to make herself believe that this lonely time was nearly over. She stared at herself in the dressing-table mirror, wondering what her mother and Linda would say about the haircut.

Joe appeared in the doorway. "Good news, huh?" He looked younger, straighter. "At least they'll be home where they belong." He glanced around the room, his jaw set against the knowledge that Linda would soon be back in her beautiful pink bed, no better off than before. "You know what I want to do to celebrate? I want to go over to the mall and look for one of those screened-in rooms for the backyard. You know, the Millikans have one."

"A gazebo?"

"Yeah, a gazebo." He repeated the word with enthusiasm. "Linda is going to need some good fresh air — she's had nothing but hospital smells for weeks. She can lie out there as long as the warm weather lasts and read or sleep or whatever." He paused. "What do you think? If we go right now, the stores will still be open."

"What about dinner?" Caroline guessed she sounded like a wet blanket, but she couldn't help it.

"Who's hungry?" Joe's grin broadened, and Caroline thought of Dwight Lloyd Boynton's advice: *Be joyous!* Joe was joyous. His joy spilled into the air around him, filling the whole house. Even the fact that Linda was still sick couldn't dim his relief, now that they were coming home.

"I'll put the food in the refrigerator," she said. "Maybe later . . ." As if they would eat warmed-over hamburgers and baked beans when they came home. It didn't matter, she told herself. The forgotten movie didn't matter either. Joe was right. The important thing was that they would soon be a family again.

The gazebo was found — to be assembled by the buyer — paid for, delivery arranged, and they were on their way home again before Caroline realized she hadn't told Joe about Mr. Jameson's fall. She brushed the thought away. Why spoil Joe's happiness by telling him someone else's problems?

But in bed that night she admitted to herself the real reason she had decided not to tell. If life was going to be just the same as it had been before Linda went away, she couldn't risk losing the trip to England. It was too much to ask. If she didn't have that to look forward to, she might turn into an invisible person again.

Chapter 14

It was easy enough to pretend that the fall hadn't happened. Mr. Jameson never mentioned it, and the walker stayed in the corner of the living room where Caroline had left it. If he used it when the nurse was there, he returned it to the corner when she left.

The first day after the fall he asked Caroline to help him sort through the contents of a clothes closet, and he had her pack away some trousers and sweaters he didn't wear anymore. The day after that they answered Jean's letter, without mentioning Mr. Jameson's health.

He's scared, Caroline guessed. He was often quiet and didn't scold as much as usual; it was as if he were saving his strength for the effort it took to walk.

Caroline could hardly bear to watch him. As he moved about the house, he hesitated for long periods, clinging to door frames and chair backs as if he didn't dare let go. *As long as he wasn't hurt, maybe it's a good thing he fell. Now he's being more careful, so it won't happen again.* The words sounded empty and wrong, but Caroline kept repeating them to herself.

The whole week was a strange one. She called Lillina to tell her Linda would be home soon, and Mrs. Reston said she was very glad to hear it but refused to call Lillina to the phone. "She has her work to do," Mrs. Reston said. She sounded disapproving. "I'll tell her you called, dear. It's good of you to be interested."

What does she mean by that? Caroline was still puzzling over the call when Joe came home from work. He had stopped at a hardware store to buy some bolts he would need to assemble Linda's gazebo. When he saw Caroline, he dropped his package on the kitchen table and shook his head teasingly.

"Good thing your mother's coming home," he said. "I never thought I'd have to worry about the company you keep. It's not easy being a father."

Caroline frowned. "What do you mean?"

"I saw Charlie Reston at the hardware store just now, and he says they're having all kinds of trouble with that redheaded friend of yours."

Caroline heard again the note of disapproval in Mrs. Reston's voice. "What kind of trouble?"

Joe poured himself a glass of water. "Charlie didn't say, and I didn't ask. It's none of my business, after all. I told him he was looking pretty solemn, and he said he had a lot to be solemn about. And then he said the girl was giving them problems." He narrowed his eyes at Caroline. "No need to get lathered, Carrie. Whatever it is, it's her worry, not yours."

Caroline turned away from him. He didn't care if Lillina was in trouble, as long as her trouble didn't touch the Cabots. He didn't care about anything except the homecoming.

"Lillina's my friend," she snapped. "The Restons don't understand her, that's all. She's too smart for them."

"I doubt that." Joe picked up the package of bolts. "I'm not kidding when I say I'm glad your mother is coming home. There's something wrong with that girl, and I don't think you should see so much of her. In the first place, she's too old for you. And in the second place, she's just plain bad news, as far as I'm concerned. She's a phony!"

Caroline clenched her fists. How could he say such things after meeting Lillina only once!

"You're different since she's been here," he went on, almost as if he were talking to himself. "You act different and you look different — "

"I thought you *liked* my haircut. You said — "

"I do like it. That's not the point. The point is, you're changing." He grinned at her, almost apologetically. "Maybe that's Lillina's doing, maybe not. I'll just be glad when your mother's back. You know, you've always been the one we didn't have to worry about. You've always been good old Caroline. . . ."

"But that's awful!" She whirled away from Joe's astonished expression and rushed out of the kitchen. Good old Caroline, indeed! Well, she was *glad* she was changing. She was sick of the old Caroline, the one no one worried about.

She stayed in her bedroom until she heard Joe go out to the backyard. The gazebo had been delivered in five huge cartons that were spread out on the lawn. They would keep him busy for a long time. Caroline wandered around the house, her thoughts racing from Lillina to Mr. Jameson to Linda — and to herself, the changed Caroline.

After a very quiet dinner, Joe settled in the living room with the newspaper and Caroline went out to the front steps. Storm clouds were piling up above the rooftops of Grand River. A lamp burned in Mr. Jameson's living room, and she could see the silver-blue glow of his television screen. As she watched, his tall silhouette lurched across the room, and then the light went on in the bathroom.

The threatening sky suited Caroline's mood. She felt restless, uneasy, lonesome. It was a relief when Lillina appeared around the side of the house. She wore black shorts and a top, with a black scarf hiding the shining hair. Her feet were bare, and her long arms and legs gleamed in the dark. She looked up and down the road quickly, then sat on the top step next to Caroline.

"What's wrong? Why did you come through the backyards? Did you finish your work?"

Lillina ignored the questions. "I have news! Marvelous news!" The gravelly voice was even more husky than usual, and the brown eyes glittered. "It's so exciting, Caroline!"

"What is?" Lillina certainly didn't sound like a person who was having problems.

"I'm going home, dear. Right away! I had a letter from Frederick, and he wants me to come at once. There are things about the house that he doesn't want to decide by himself. And besides, he misses me terribly. . . . Not only that, Caroline. In the very same mail, I had a letter from the Jill Compton Modeling Agency, and they want me to come in for an interview right away. Isn't that just fantastic?"

"What about your mother and dad?" Caroline asked. "Didn't you promise them you'd stay here all summer?" This must be the problem Mr. Reston had meant: Lillina wanted to go home sooner than originally planned. And she had an appointment with a big, important modeling agency. The Restons would think that was a problem, too.

"My parents will understand." Lillina fluttered her fingers, a dismissing gesture. "They'll see that I have to get on with my life."

Get on with my life. Caroline said the words over to herself. She liked the way they sounded. Maybe, she thought, that was what was happening to her this summer. She wasn't just changing; she was getting on with her life.

"When are you going?"

Lillina pointed one foot like a ballerina. "In the next few days — I'm not quite sure when. But we'll keep in touch, Caroline. I'll have so much to tell you. I'll want to hear what you're doing, of course, and how your sister is — "

"She's coming home!" Caroline had almost forgotten to tell her own good news. "She and my mom will be here sometime this weekend."

Lillina threw her arms around Caroline and hugged her. "That's wonderful, dear. Is she cured?"

"No. She might be a little bit better, though. Joe's building a gazebo for her in the backyard."

"I saw it." Lillina looked thoughtful. "What does he say about your trip to England?"

Caroline squirmed. "I haven't talked to him about it yet," she admitted. "He and my mom know Jeannie invited me, and they know Grandma said she'd buy the airplane ticket, but I think they've forgotten all that by now."

"Remind them," Lillina said promptly. "If it was Eleanor, she'd want to get the date settled as soon as possible."

Caroline knew that was true. Eleanor was the kind of person who would speak up when she had something on her mind; she wouldn't keep putting it off. By this time, she would have told Joe she had almost enough money saved for the trip to England. She would have told him that Mr. Jameson had fallen because he was too stubborn and too proud to use a walker. Mr. Jameson . . . had been in the bathroom a very long time! Caroline's stomach churned as she realized how long that light had been on. He couldn't be taking a shower; he did that in the morning when the visiting nurse was there.

She jumped up. "I have to go across the street for a minute," she said. "I have to make sure Mr. Jameson is okay." She dashed across

Barker Road, her heart thumping, and was fumbling with Mr. Jameson's front door before she realized Lillina was beside her.

"He'll be angry if there's nothing wrong," Caroline warned as she pushed open the door and stepped inside. "He hates having people worry about him. . . ."

Lillina retreated. "Then maybe we shouldn't bother him. What makes you think — "

Caroline moved farther inside. Mr. Jameson was her job. In a totally unexpected way he was even, she realized suddenly, her friend. Friends had a right to check on each other.

"You can stay here if you want to," she said. "I'm going to knock on the bathroom door and ask him if he's all right."

As soon as she turned from the living room into the hall, she knew the answer to her question. The bathroom door was open. Two trousered legs extended from the bathroom halfway across the hall carpet.

"Mr. Jameson?" Her throat ached with the effort it took to say his name.

There was no answer.

Chapter 15

"Is he dead?"

Lillina peered into the bathroom. She looked as if she were about to faint.

Caroline knelt beside Mr. Jameson and pressed a finger to his throat, the way she'd seen doctors do on television. The skin was papery, cool but not cold. A pulse flickered under her touch.

"No," she said in a strangled voice. "But there's blood on his forehead and on the floor." She bent close to the old man's bristly gray-white face. "Mr. Jameson? Can you hear me? What happened?"

He didn't move. She became aware of harsh, shallow breaths that gradually grew louder, like snores.

"Call an ambulance, quick." She looked over her shoulder at Lillina, who hovered in the hall like a tall marsh bird ready for flight.

"I — I can't." Lillina stared down at Mr. Jameson. "I don't know who to call. You do it, Caroline."

"The operator! Just tell the operator!" Caroline paused, forcing herself to think. "No, wait. The visiting nurse taped an emergency number to the telephone. Call that. The phone is in the kitchen."

Lillina still didn't move.

"Hurry up!" Caroline ordered. "He's breathing so funny — I don't know what's happening."

Like someone walking in her sleep, Lillina moved down the hall to the kitchen. Her voice shook as she gave the message; she sounded like a frightened child.

"Mr. Jameson. Please wake up. *Please!*" Caroline touched the bony hand. She felt his throat again, and it seemed to her that his pulse was weaker than it had been before.

Lillina returned. She was shivering, though the house was sticky-hot. "The paramedics are coming right away," she said. "Has he said anything?"

Caroline shook her head. She was very close to tears. "He must have lost his balance when he reached for the light switch," she said. "He's been lying here all this time *bleeding*."

"Well, it isn't your fault," Lillina said, sounding a little more like herself. She knelt next to Caroline. "Poor old man. It must be terrible to have nobody care what happens to you."

"He has a very nice niece in Missouri," Caroline said sharply. "She loves him a lot. And he has me." *But I let him go on stumbling around the house without his walker, when I knew darned well he might fall.*

"Well, of course, dear." Lillina stood up and went back to the living room. Caroline would have liked to follow her and wait for the ambulance there, but she couldn't leave Mr. Jameson by himself. *He has me*, she repeated to herself.

With the arrival of the ambulance, the house seemed to fill up with people. Joe was one of the first to arrive. "You should have called me, Carrie," he said. "I didn't even know you'd left the house."

"I didn't stop to think," Caroline explained. "I saw the bathroom light, and it didn't go off — so I just ran over here. After I found him I didn't want to leave. I was afraid he'd wake up and think he was still alone."

They moved into the kitchen, keeping out of the way while the paramedics worked over their patient. Lillina and Mrs. Kramer and the Millikans were there, too, Lillina standing by herself near the window. Caroline looked down at the note pad positioned precisely beneath the telephone. The Cabots' number was there, and beneath it the number of the visiting nurse.

"I should call Mrs. Morton," she said. "Otherwise she'll come tomorrow morning and wonder where Mr. Jameson is."

"Good thinking." Joe nodded approval, and listened while she made the call. Mrs. Morton said she would check with the hospital in the morning and find out how Mr. Jameson was, then call Caroline. She promised to notify his niece, too, and the housekeeper who came to fix his dinner in the evening.

"It's lucky you were watching, Caroline," she said warmly. "He should be grateful to you, and I know he will be. He's very fond of you."

The paramedics appeared, guiding the stretcher toward the front door. Caroline hurried after them, and Joe and the neighbors followed.

"He looks dead," Mrs. Kramer whispered. "Poor soul."

"It's going to rain any minute," Mrs. Millikan announced. "They'd better hurry with that stretcher."

At the curb, Caroline bent one more time over the beaky face. "Mr. Jameson, it's Caroline. Can you hear me?"

"Better move back," Joe said gently and put his arm around her shoulder. The stretcher was swung up into the ambulance, and a minute later the flashing red light moved down Barker Road. Caroline had the same lost sensation she'd known when Linda was taken to the hospital at the beginning of summer vacation.

"Well, that's that," Joe murmured. "I hope he'll be all right."

"So do I." Caroline's voice trembled, and Joe looked at her sharply.

"Want me to go back in there with you to lock up?"

She shook her head. "I'll be home in a few minutes," she said.

She looked for Lillina and decided she must have left when the stretcher was carried out. That was all right. Caroline wanted to be by herself for a while.

The neat little house had an abandoned air. Caroline went into the living room and straightened the pillow on Mr. Jameson's television-watching chair. Then she wandered out to the kitchen. It was spotlessly neat except for a cup which she washed, dried, and put back in the cupboard. *Now everything's ready for him to come home,* she thought. It was a little like a prayer. *When he comes home. Tomorrow. Or the next day.*

A floorboard creaked in the back of the house. Caroline swallowed hard. *All old houses make noises,* she told herself. *There's no one here but me.* But she tiptoed down the hall, just in case. The bathroom light was still on, the bedroom dark. She had reached the bathroom doorway and was trying to force herself to go on when Lillina stepped out of the bedroom.

Caroline squealed with fright. "I thought — " She blinked at the tall figure, a ghostly wraith in black shorts, shirt, and scarf.

Lillina stood very still. Her arms were folded tightly under her skimpy breasts. "I was just checking the windows, Caroline. I wanted to do *something* for that poor man. Everything is locked now. . . ."

"Good." They stared at each other. Lillina took a step forward, but Caroline didn't move out of her way.

"I have to go home," Lillina said. "Aunt Louise will wonder where I am. She worries so."

"She knew you were coming over to my house, didn't she?" Caroline's voice was cold.

"Well, of course, dear. But it was just to be for a few minutes — to tell you all my good news. Ever since that silly business with the Kramers' dog, she frets about my going out at night." She took another step.

"I don't believe you." Caroline reached out and pulled, hard, on one of Lillina's clasped arms.

"What's the matter with you, Caroline?" Lillina backed away quickly, but not quickly enough. A shower of bills fluttered from the bottom of her shirt.

Both girls stared at the money scattered on the floor. "I knew it," Caroline said dully. "I knew it when you came out of the bedroom. That's Mr. Jameson's money. You're stealing from a poor, sick, old man."

"No!" For a minute, Lillina appeared as shocked as Caroline felt. "How can you say that, dear? I was just — I would never — "

"Yes, you would! You did!" Caroline wanted to scream her outrage at this betrayal, but the events of the last hour had left her drained. She could only stand there in the hall, looking at Lillina.

Lillina the thief.

"How did you know where his money was?" But as she asked the question, she remembered the night she'd sat on the front steps with Joe and told him about the cash in the dresser drawer. Lillina had been standing silently at the corner of the front yard. *What in heck is that?* Joe had asked when they finally saw her there.

"You heard me telling Joe." Caroline answered herself.

Lillina shoved Caroline out of her way and ran down the hall. More bills fluttered behind her.

"I hate you!" Caroline shouted after her. "I hate anybody who'd steal from a helpless person. You were right last Sunday when you said you made mistakes. . . ."

The screen door slammed. Caroline leaned against the wall, trembling. After a moment, she got down on the floor and gathered up the scattered bills. They were mostly fifties and twenties. She went into the bedroom and switched on the light. The top dresser drawer was open, the stationery box lying on the dresser next to Mr. Jameson's brush and comb. A few bills remained in the drawer.

She lifted out the stationery and put the money into the box. Lillina wouldn't have another chance at it, and neither would anyone else. *I let him fall, but I won't let anyone take his money*, she thought fiercely. She hurried through the house, checking the back door and the windows, turning off the remaining lights.

When she got home, Joe was in the kitchen. "I was just coming over to see where you were," he said. "What took so long?"

"I decided to bring Mr. Jameson's money home with me," Caroline told him. "Someone could break in and take it while he's away." She laid the stationery box on the table.

Joe started to protest, but her expression stopped him. "Well, I see your point," he said slowly. "Not that I like having charge of his money without his permission. I'll take it down to the bank first thing tomorrow and open an account in his name, okay?" He studied Caroline with concern. "You've had quite an evening, haven't you? How about some warm milk to relax?"

"Yuk!"

"Cocoa, maybe?"

"I don't think so." She was more tired than she could ever remember being before. Joe was right; it had been quite an evening, and he didn't even know what Lillina had tried to do. "I guess I'll just go to bed."

Joe nodded. "You handled yourself pretty darned well tonight. It was smart to notice that Jameson's bathroom light stayed on too long. And you got help for the old man in a hurry. Your mother's going to be proud of you when she hears about it."

For just a moment, Caroline let herself enjoy his praise. It was true she'd helped Mr. Jameson when he needed it. She'd taken charge and hadn't panicked. She hadn't been good old Caroline, waiting for someone to tell her what to do. But her good feelings about herself didn't last. Mr. Jameson probably wouldn't be in the hospital now if she'd alerted Joe, or the visiting nurse, to the fact that he refused to use his walker. What possible excuse did she have for keeping quiet, except the worst excuse of all: *I didn't want to lose my job.*

"I just hope he's okay," she said. " 'Night, Joe."

"Good night."

She was in her bedroom, pulling her T-shirt over her head, when Joe called to her again. "Meant to tell you, Louise Reston called. Wanted to know if that girl — what's-her-name — was here. Said she'd left the house without telling them. I told her about Jameson, and I said I saw the kid over there. She must have wandered in with all the rest of the neighbors."

"Okay. Thanks." Caroline climbed into bed and pulled the sheet up to her chin.

So Lillina had lied about having permission to go out, just as Caroline had suspected. She was a sneak as well as a thief, and Caroline hoped they'd never meet again.

Raindrops pelted the window, and thunder rumbled in the distance. Caroline couldn't hold back her tears any longer. She cried for Mr. Jameson, who might be dead at this very minute. Then she cried for the friendship that had made this whole long summer interesting and had been destroyed in five ugly minutes. The rain covered the sounds of her sobs and eventually put her to sleep.

Chapter 16

It was raining lightly when Caroline woke to the ring of the telephone. She felt as if she'd been sleeping for years. Her head was heavy, and she longed to slide back into sleep even before she remembered the events of the night before.

The phone kept ringing. Either Joe was sleeping later than usual because it was Saturday, or he was already out in the backyard in the rain, putting the finishing touches on the gazebo. Caroline slid out of bed and stumbled down the hall to the phone in Linda's room.

"Caroline Cabot?" It was the visiting nurse, Mrs. Morton. "I just wanted to let you know that Mr. Jameson is ever so much better this morning. . . ."

Caroline realized she'd been holding her breath. "Oh, good!" she exclaimed. *Good, a thousand times, a million times over!*

"He may have a concussion," Mrs. Morton hurried on, "so they want to keep him in the hospital for a while and watch him. But he's awake, and he's growling at the nurses, so he must feel like himself." She chuckled. "I've called his niece. She was very concerned — he never even told her about the stroke last winter. She's coming up here as soon as she can find someone to look after her children." She paused. "Are you still there, Caroline?"

"Oh, yes."

"Well, I think it's likely the niece will invite him to come to Missouri to live with her. And I for one think it would be a fine idea. I have this feeling that Mr. Jameson doesn't use his walker as much as he should. He can be a very naughty boy, you know. Did you notice whether he had the walker with him when he fell?"

Caroline squirmed. "I guess he didn't."

"Just as I thought. Well, no use fretting about it now, I suppose. Anyway, I left a message with the floor nurse. I told her to tell Mr. Jameson that you were the person who found him and called for help. I thought he should know that."

Joe came in from the backyard just as they were saying good-bye. Caroline told him the good news.

"That's great," Joe said. "And what about

you? You looked pretty shaken up when you went to bed."

"I'm better, too." At least, she was better than she'd been last night. Knowing Mr. Jameson was going to be all right had taken a tremendous weight off her shoulders. It even made her a little less angry with Lillina.

The telephone rang again before they sat down to breakfast. This time Joe answered it. He listened for a moment, then called Caroline. "It's Louise Reston." He was obviously irritated. "Something about that kid again."

Caroline picked up the phone cautiously, as if it might burn her fingers.

"Caroline, would you come over here, dear? I must talk to you." Mrs. Reston sounded as if she were crying.

"I — I don't know if I can." She glanced at Joe, who was listening from the doorway. Going to the Reston house was the last thing she wanted to do, and she knew Joe would refuse permission if she asked him.

"Please, dear. It's very important."

Caroline wished she could snap her fingers and fly away. *To England,* she thought. *I wish I were with Jeannie in London right this minute.*

"Lillina won't want to see me," she told Mrs. Reston. "We had — a kind of argument last night." Joe's eyebrows shot up.

"But that's the point!" Mrs. Reston exclaimed. "Lillian isn't here, Caroline. She left this morning, and I just don't know where to start looking for her. She was very upset, and so was I. I thought, since you know her so well —"

But I don't really know her. I thought I did, but I don't.

"Do you mean she left because of our fight?"

"No, no, no! I don't know anything about that. Caroline, this is very serious. Won't you please —"

Caroline gave up. "Okay," she said, careful to avoid Joe's eyes. "I guess I can come for a little while."

Joe waited for her to hang up. "I told you I didn't want you to see so much of that girl," he snapped. "Can't you tell she's trouble?"

"Lillina's not there," Caroline explained. "Besides, I think she's going to go home in a few days — maybe right away. Mrs. Reston just wants to talk to me."

"Well, I don't like it." He shoved his hands into his pockets and scowled. "I was counting on you to do some housecleaning today. I don't want your mother to come home and start right in working."

Caroline felt as if she were being pulled, hard, in two directions. "I'll just be gone for a little while," she said lamely. "I have to go, Joe."

He sighed. "Then that's it, I suppose. But you can tell that woman for me, I hope she doesn't have any more houseguests for a long, long time."

He stomped down the hall to the kitchen. Caroline hesitated a moment, then decided to forget breakfast and get the visit to Mrs. Reston over with as quickly as possible.

What would Eleanor do? After all, Eleanor was Lillina's sister and would be even more upset than Caroline was. What would she *do*? Asking the question had become a useful sort of habit. It helped to have a friend who knew how to face up to problems.

Eleanor would try to stay calm. She'd be understanding. She'd keep her feelings about Lillina to herself.

By the time Caroline reached the Restons' front door, she had a plan. She would explain, as quickly as possible, that she couldn't even guess where Lillina might be. She would tell Mrs. Reston that she and Lillina weren't close anymore, without saying why. And then she'd hurry home and concentrate on getting ready for the homecoming. She would clean the house. Pick flowers for Linda's bedside table. Make brownies.

"Caroline!" Mrs. Reston, red-eyed and shiny-cheeked, looked as if she would like to wrap Caroline in a hug. "Oh, I'm so glad you could come. My husband is away for the whole weekend — a lodge convention — and I just don't know what to do. Come in, dear."

Caroline's courage began to dissolve in the face of this desperate-sounding welcome. Reluctantly, she followed Mrs. Reston into the stuffy, overfurnished living room.

"Look at this!" Mrs. Reston thrust two envelopes into Caroline's hand. "Read the letters," she urged. "Read them before we talk."

The letters were addressed to modeling agencies in New York City. Except for the addresses, they were identical. Each of them said that Lillina MacGregor would be arriving in the city next week and requested an appointment.

"Lillina MacGregor is Lillian," Mrs. Reston explained unnecessarily. "Our Lillian Taylor! Making appointments — in New York! What do you think of that?"

"Well, she told me she's going home soon," Caroline said, trying to sound calm and understanding. "I guess she thought as long as she was going back to New York, she'd better get started on her career — "

"Whatever are you saying?" Mrs. Reston sank down on the sofa. She dabbed at her eyes with a wad of tissues. "What do you mean, *back to New York?* She's going home, all right, as fast as I can get her there, but home is a long way from New York. Her home is in Graham, Michigan. The Upper Peninsula. The closest Graham's ever come to a model is in the Sears catalog. I ought to know — I was born there."

Caroline stared at her.

"What has that girl been telling you, anyway? Has she been filling you with a lot of lies about herself? I wouldn't put it past her. You know, if we'd had any idea what we were getting into, we never would have let her mother send her to us. If we'd known she was a thief — "

"A thief!" Caroline jumped. Had Lillina told Mrs. Reston about last night?

"Yes, a thief," Mrs. Reston repeated. "There've been at least three times that she's taken money from us. Mr. Reston is the treasurer of his lodge, you see, and he's missed money a couple of times. We knew Lillian took it — she was the only one who could have done it. We made her stay in her room as punishment. But she never admitted what she'd done — not for a minute!" Mrs. Reston shrugged angrily. "This morning I actually caught her in the act. She knew I'd taken money from the bank for a shopping trip, and she had her hand in my purse when I happened to walk into the bedroom. . . ." She wiped her eyes again. "I don't like to ship her home, but I'm going to do it. I won't have a person like that in this house. I can't stand it. Our girls never gave us such problems."

Caroline looked down at the letters in her lap.

"She even used my best stationery to write those silly things," Mrs. Reston said, following her glance. "She even stole *that!* I never saw a girl so determined to become something she's not and never will be."

"But —" Caroline didn't know what to say. Lillina and New York belonged together.

"It's disgusting!" Mrs. Reston spoke with an intensity that made Caroline flinch. "All that child thinks about is being famous. She can't just take snapshots — not her! She has to be a big, important portrait artist. And glamorous! I swear, she thinks she's gorgeous! She actually believes she's going to take this whole world by storm, and all of us ordinary folks are going to tell her how wonderful she is. You've seen that, Caroline. You know it for a fact."

Caroline cleared her throat, but before she could think of a calm, understanding reply, Mrs. Reston was talking again.

"She's smart as a whip, I don't deny that. But I bet she didn't tell you she's failing every single class in high school. Her teachers gave her homework to do all summer, so she could catch up, and I've done my best to make her study, but I don't think she's accomplished a thing. She just sits and dreams, or reads those fashion magazines. She's a — a collector, that's what she is! Picks up ideas and pretends all the time. Makes a fairy-tale kind of life for herself! And now this!" She pointed at the letters. "Last night she sneaked out of the house, so I went to her room and found these and read them. When she came home, I told her just what I thought. And then this morning I caught her taking money from my purse. When she realized she'd been caught, she ran right out of the house. . . . Where would she go, Caroline? You don't have to worry about getting her into more trouble than she's already in. All I want is to find her and pack her up and send her back to Graham, as fast as I can."

Caroline struggled with this torrent of new information. "Do you mean," she said slowly, "that Lillina is still in high school?"

"Of course she's in high school. She'll be a sophomore this year. *If* she makes up her work. Didn't she even tell you the truth about that, for heaven's sake?"

"I never asked her about school," Caroline said. "When she said she was married, I just thought . . ." She hesitated. Mrs. Reston looked about to choke. "His name is Frederick — "

"Married!" The word was like a small explosion. "She's not *married*. Just exactly how old did she say she is?"

"Seventeen," Caroline whispered.

"Fifteen is more like it. Married, indeed! A gawky fifteen, if you want the truth. My girls had some meat on their bones. The idea of that child imagining herself glamorous!"

Caroline thought of the afternoon she and Lillina had spent at the mall. She remembered Lillina in the black dress and later in the yellow one, her mane of red hair flung back, radiant in a way that had taken Caroline's breath away. *Lillina really is beautiful, Mrs. Reston,* she wanted to say. Then she thought about how that afternoon had ended, with a flash of green that might have been a stolen bracelet.

"Why did she come to Grand River?"

Mrs. Reston sniffed. "Because I offered to see what I could do with her. Her dear mama was my best friend in school. She works, and Lillian was on her own most of the time. The father's dead long ago, and they're dirt-poor — live in a house that's hardly more than a shack, near Lake Superior.

"Her mama's been trying to get Lillian to think about a business course so she can get a job and help out as soon as she's out of school. But she hasn't been doing *any* schoolwork at all. Just talked big and chased after boys, till finally her mama decided maybe if she got away to a different place for a while..." Mrs. Reston leaned her bulk against the sofa cushions. "She knew my girls never had a bit of nonsense about them, and so she thought maybe I could do something with Lillian. But I can't work miracles. And if Lillian was stealing at home and I wasn't told, well, I call that a dirty trick."

Caroline stood up shakily. She didn't want to hear any more. "I don't know where she is, Mrs. Reston," she said. "I'm sorry — I promised my stepfather I'd come right home, so — "

Tears welled again in Mrs. Reston's eyes. Her expression softened, and suddenly Caroline realized that she was frightened as well as angry. "The thing is, dear, I believe I *might* have hurt the girl's feelings." She looked at Caroline pleadingly. "She made me so mad — the stealing and all that silliness about going to New York. I told her right out — "

Caroline looked away. She didn't want to hear this, but she couldn't move.

" — I told her she was too plain and too lazy to be a big, glamorous success at anything. I told her she'd better stop hurting her mama and think about making herself useful in the world." The wad of tissue appeared again. "I don't usually talk like that. I was mean! But she made me wild!"

The stinging words echoed in Caroline's ears, drowning out Mrs. Reston's soft sobs. Poor Lillina! No wonder she'd run away!

"Caroline, dear, she's such a strange girl. You don't think she'd — she'd *hurt* herself, do you?"

" — I don't know." Caroline gulped as Mrs. Reston's broad face crumpled. "No — no, I'm sure Lillina wouldn't do anything like that."

But would she? Caroline felt as if she were going to be sick.

"You'll call me if you hear from her?"

"Yes, I will. But I have to go now. I really have to. . . ."

Outside at last, she threw back her head and let the mist cool her hot face. *I don't have to do anything except go home*, she told herself. *After last night Lillina doesn't want to see me again, and I don't want to see her. I don't! Even if I knew where she was . . .*"

There was one possibility. Caroline knew where Lillina had seemed happiest — where she just might go to get back the dream Mrs. Reston had tried to banish. But it was only a possibility, and Joe was waiting at home. By tomorrow, with her mother and Linda back in Grand River, Lillina could be just a painful memory.

Go home, she told herself. *Why bother with someone who's been lying to you all summer?*

It was raining harder now as she stood there trying to make up her mind. Her feet were wet, her bangs were flattened across her forehead, and she felt very much like the old beginning-of-the-summer Caroline. Eventually, though, the question presented itself in a familiar way.

What would Eleanor do?

Chapter 17

"Oh, yes, she was here."

The saleswoman at Margo's Fashions was not the same one who had helped them the day Caroline and Lillina had come to the mall together. This woman was small and dark, her face set in resentful lines. She looked as if she might have missed her bus that morning or spilled her coffee or broken a fingernail. Maybe all three.

"Is she — " Caroline glanced toward the dressing rooms.

"I said she *was* here. She picked out at least five dresses she wanted to try on, and then while I was finding the last one in her size, she just disappeared. Walked out without a word." The woman narrowed her eyes at the mall entrance, as if Lillina might still be lingering there. "I should have known better. When she walked in, I was afraid she was just one of those brassy kids who didn't have any intention of buying, but you can never be sure. . . ." She transferred the glare to Caroline. "A friend of yours, I suppose. How old is she, anyway?"

Caroline backed up a step. "I — I'm not sure. I have to find her — "

"Well, she's not here." The woman turned away. "And when you find her, you tell her this is a store for adults. We don't appreciate children coming in to play games."

Back in the noisy, brightly lit mall, Caroline wondered what to do next. Margo's Fashions had been the one place she could think of where Lillina might go. And it had been a good guess. But Lillina had left without trying on any of the beautiful dresses — without becoming, for a few minutes, the model of her fantasies.

Bradens' Department Store was a short way down the mall. There were only one or two shoppers at the jewelry counter, both of them white-haired. Caroline hadn't really expected to find Lillina there. If she'd actually stolen a bracelet, she wouldn't return to the scene of the crime, would she?

Caroline went out the south door of the mall and started back toward the bus stop. By this time, Joe had probably called Mrs. Reston to say Caroline must come home at once. He'd be furious when he discovered she wasn't there. Maybe he'd even think she'd been kidnapped as she walked along Barker Road. Or maybe — she giggled a little hysterically — he would decide the Kramers' dog had eaten her up. Or maybe he wasn't concerned at all! He didn't like the new Caroline as well as the old one — he'd practically said so. Perhaps with Linda coming home tomorrow, he would feel that one daughter — the perfect one — was enough.

A mean thought! She peered down the road, but the bus wasn't in sight. She ought to call Joe and tell him where she was. He'd be angry with her, but at least he could stop worrying. She looked around for a public telephone, and her eyes fell on the big neon sign beyond the highway.

The Talbott Inn.

Halfway across the parking lot, Caroline began to run. Suddenly she felt as if she were inside Lillina's head and knew what she was feeling. Lillina had been too upset to try on the dresses at Margo's Fashions, and besides, it wouldn't have been as satisfying if there had been no one but a suspicious saleswoman to watch and admire her. Better to find someplace else where she could be the glamorous person she wanted to be.

Caroline hurried across the lobby of the Inn, with only a quick glance through the door of the coffee shop. At the archway leading into the dining room, she stopped. Dim, recessed lights made it hard to see across the restaurant, and at first she thought the room was empty except for a couple of tables of businessmen lingering over late-breakfast coffee. Then, her eyes becoming accustomed to the soft light, she saw that a diner sat alone at a table near the center of the room, studying a menu. As Caroline watched, the menu was laid aside, revealing red hair, slanting eyes, and a haughty expression.

"I'm meeting my friend over there," Caroline said to the hostess behind the stand-up desk. The hostess nodded coolly. She probably wasn't used to having kids come in without their parents.

As she made her way across the room, Caroline half expected Lillina to get up and run away from her, the way she'd been running ever since last night. But Lillina's smile was brilliant and welcoming. "Caroline dear," she said kindly, as if there had been no furious exchange in Mr. Jameson's hallway. Or as if she'd decided to forgive Caroline for believing the worst. "Whatever are you doing here?"

"Looking for you," Caroline said bluntly. She pulled out a red velvet chair and sat down. "I can't order anything. I only have enough money for the bus fare home."

Lillina leaned toward her. The brown eyes glittered unnaturally, and her cheeks were flushed a bright pink under their freckles. "Don't worry about that, dear," she said. "Order anything you want. Absolutely anything! My treat, of course. I'm going to have a marvelous early lunch myself, to celebrate my going home. Frederick sent me far more money than necessary again this week — "

"There isn't any Frederick," Caroline said. "You've been taking Mr. Reston's lodge money, haven't you?"

Lillina shivered. The bright smile slipped away for a second and then returned. "What *are* you talking about, Caroline? Frederick is my husband. He's the most wonderful — "

"You're fifteen years old," Caroline gritted. "You're going to be a terrific model someday, but right now you're a sophomore in high school. There isn't any novel either, is there? You've been doing make-up homework when you said you were writing a book."

A waitress, trim in black and white, appeared between them. Lillina snatched up the menu and studied it. "The lobster salad sounds divine," she said. "And maybe — yes, the cold consommé first. And a carafe of white wine would be nice. Chablis, please."

The waitress appeared uneasy as she tried to decide whether Lillina was as old as she sounded.

"I'd like a glass of milk, please," Caroline

said, and blushed. Maybe they didn't even serve milk in a sophisticated restaurant like this one.

The waitress still hesitated. "Thank you," she said finally, and retreated.

Caroline turned back to Lillina. "You don't live in New York, you live in Michigan," she said. "In a little town near Lake Superior. You've never been to New York in your whole life."

Lillina's long fingers twisted knots in her linen napkin. "Caroline, how can you say things like that? Such terrible things!" Head high, eyes brighter than ever, she was, no matter what Mrs. Reston said, beautiful.

"I'm not mad at you," Caroline said. "You're my friend." And that was true, too. All the way to the mall she'd stared out the bus window and tried to see the world as Lillina saw it. She had tried hard to understand. "I think you *have* to make things up," she said. "You don't like who you are and so you pretend to be someone else you like better."

The light drained from Lillina's eyes. She leaned back in the velvet chair. "I thought *you* liked me," she said slowly. "Somebody's been telling you lies."

Caroline brushed her bangs back from her forehead. "I do like you. I like you the way you really are, Lillina. I just want to get things straight between us. *You've* been telling me a pack of lies all summer."

"I thought you liked me," Lillina repeated. "I thought you and Eleanor and I — "

Caroline bit her lip. This was the worst part. "There's no Eleanor either," she said softly. "Don't tell me about her anymore, because she isn't real."

"She *is*, Caroline! Eleanor is my little sister who's just like you."

Caroline shook her head. "I saw your aunt Louise's stationery — the paper you used to write those letters to the modeling agencies. It's pale gray — the same color and the same size as Eleanor's. You wrote those letters to me, Lillina."

There it was. Caroline held her breath, longing to hear something that would make Eleanor live again. She didn't care about Frederick — she'd never been absolutely sure there was a Frederick — but Eleanor was different. Eleanor had been an important part of this summer.

"Why did you do that?" she demanded when Lillina just stared at her. "I guess I understand about the other stuff, but why did you make up Eleanor?"

"Because you were my friend!" Lillina said impatiently. "I wanted to give you someone. Someone to be like, do you see? You should be glad, Caroline. Eleanor's a really special person." She frowned, as if this ought to be enough explanation for any reasonable person.

So that was it, Caroline thought. *Eleanor was a gift. Lillina had already made up the kind of person she wanted to be herself, and then she thought up a make-believe Caroline — the kind of person I might be if I wanted to try.* Perfectly logical, from Lillina's point of view.

She sighed. "Mrs. Reston is worried about you," she said. "You'd better call her."

And Joe! What was Joe thinking by this time?

"I don't want to talk to her!" Lillina sounded desperate. "She doesn't like me, Caroline. Lots of grownups don't. Aunt Louise despises me. Why should I call her?"

The waitress returned and set Lillina's soup in front of her. It was clear and golden, in a delicate bowl set on a lace doily.

"I don't want that," Lillina said. "You can take it away."

The waitress stared at her and then looked across the table at Caroline. "I've changed my mind, that's all," Lillina snapped. "I'm not hungry. You can forget the lobster salad, too."

"But — "

Lillina opened her big shoulder bag and took out a roll of bills. She peeled away several dollars and threw them on the tablecloth.

"That should be enough," she said. "That's plenty." She hurled the rest of the money at Caroline. "You can take that to Aunt Louise," she cried. "Tell her she can have it back — I don't need it. I can get to New York by myself. I'm going to be famous, no matter what she thinks or what you think!" She was on her feet, screaming. "It's not a lie! It's not!"

The waitress stood frozen. Caroline saw the hostess darting toward them.

"Girls!" The hostess spoke in a shocked whisper. "Stop this immediately! The idea — "

"I don't know what's the matter with her," the waitress complained. "She just started in, all of a sudden. I think she's crazy or something!"

Lillina gave an anguished moan and leapt away from the hostess's restraining hand. "Let me alone!" she shrieked. "Don't you touch me! Someday you'll all be sorry — "

She ran across the dining room, bumping into tables and sobbing. For a moment, Caroline was too appalled to move. Then she bent down and started scooping up the bills that had fallen on the floor around her.

"You'd better go after her," the hostess said. "She's hysterical. I never saw such a terrible display — "

There was a crash in the lobby. Caroline started to run, with the hostess and the waitress right behind her. From the corner of her eye, she saw two of the businessmen get up and follow them.

The elegant lobby was a shambles. From every doorway, people were pouring into the room. At its center, Lillina lay sprawled on the floor, long legs stretched in front of her. The pedestal that held the big metal urn had been knocked over, and the urn had rolled across the floor. Its contents — a quantity of dried flowers — had landed in Lillina's lap, almost covering her with a prickly blanket of gold and orange and green. A long yellow blossom rose stiffly, like an Indian feather, from the mane of red hair.

Don't let them laugh at her, Caroline prayed. It was a real prayer, as heartfelt as the prayers she'd said in church last Sunday. She had a feeling that Lillina really would go crazy if anyone laughed.

She needn't have worried. There was nothing but outrage in the faces of the hostess and the hotel manager as they pushed through the crowd and lifted Lillina to her feet.

"Just look what you've done!" the hostess scolded. "If that vase is damaged, your parents will have to pay for it. What's your name?"

Lillina didn't answer. She looked around vaguely, as if puzzled to find herself the center of so much commotion.

Caroline slipped her arm around Lillina's waist. "My name is Caroline Cabot," she told the hostess. "We're very sorry about the vase. If you could let me use a telephone, I'll call the people my friend is staying with — "

"I want her name and address," the manager interrupted. "Neither of you leaves here till we know who you are and find out how much damage has been done."

Caroline's face burned with embarrassment. "Come on, Lillina," she whispered. "It'll be okay." The crowd moved back, and the girls followed the manager across the lobby to his office.

"I don't want Aunt Louise to come," Lillina wailed. "Don't call her, Caroline. Please!"

The manager took their names and addresses, then left them sitting on the couch in his office. When he came back, he seemed a little less glum. "The urn has a couple of small dents — nothing serious." He looked at Lillina, who was crying softly. "You can go now," he said. "And please don't come back unless your parents come with you."

The thought of taking a bus home with Lillina in her present state was a dismaying one. "I have to call my stepfather," Caroline said. By this time, Joe would be both worried and angry; the last thing he'd want to do was rescue Lillina from one of her "problems." But there was no one else, and so, with the manager listening and Lillina sniffing softly in the background, she dialed her house.

"Joe, I'm with Lillina at the mall, and we need help," she said. The words tumbled out before Joe could start to scold.

There was the briefest of pauses. "Are *you* okay, Carrie?"

She turned away so the manager couldn't see the tears welling in her own eyes. "Yes. But we're at the Talbott Inn, and there's been a sort of — sort of accident. Can you come — "

"I'll be right there." The phone clicked sharply in her ear.

"He's coming," Caroline said. She felt lightheaded with relief. "We'll wait out in front for him."

"That's not nesessary." The manager was watching Lillina warily now. It had occurred to him, as it had to Caroline, that she might become hysterical again. "You'd better stay with her. Maybe she'll feel better if she rests awhile." He went out, with a backward glance that said as clearly as words that he wanted to be somewhere else if there was to be another explosion.

For more than twenty minutes the girls sat quietly in the little office and waited. Lillina's sobs gradually faded, but she spoke only twice.

"My name really is Lillina," she said

abruptly. "It's not just a mistake on my birth certificate, no matter what my mother and Aunt Louise say. Don't you think it's a lovely name, Caroline?"

"Yes, I do." Caroline discovered she had goosebumps, even though the office was stuffy.

The next time Lillina spoke was when they heard Joe's voice in the lobby, asking where his stepdaughter was. Caroline started to get up, and Lillina clung to her wrist. "You really took care of everything very nicely, dear," she said. The smile came back, glittering through tears. "You handled that man just the way Eleanor would have done."

"If there were an Eleanor," Caroline said softly.

And Lillina said, "Of course, dear. If there were an Eleanor."

Chapter 18

It was a lovely day for the homecoming — bright and warm, with a breeze that set the petunias and snapdragons dancing. Caroline and Joe ate their lunch in the new gazebo.

"Not a bad omelet," Joe teased. "If you like 'em a little dry." He tried to look serious, but his eyes were shining and the corners of his mouth twitched.

Caroline took a bite of her omelet. "*I* think it's perfect," she said firmly. "Absolutely perfect! I may go into the omelet-making business."

Joe shook his head. "What conceit! I never thought you were like that, kiddo. I never thought good old Caroline — " He stopped, realizing he was on dangerous ground.

But Caroline pretended not to hear. "Do you know what else I'm going to do this fall?" she asked. "Besides learn to cook lots of new things? I'm going to enter my dollhouse furniture in the Grand River hobby fair. I never did that before. I bet I'll get a ribbon."

Joe grinned. "I wouldn't be surprised if you did," he agreed. "You've had quite a summer. Not exactly boring, huh?"

Caroline glowed. *Not boring at all,* she thought. This morning Mr. Jameson had called to ask her if she'd check the house each day while he was in the hospital. He had some errands he wanted her to run, too, and he suggested that she might want to come to visit him. He'd spoken as if she were a grownup. And a friend.

"Still, that was pretty irresponsible yesterday," Joe went on, as if he could read her mind. "Don't you ever run off like that again without telling your mother or me where you're going, Carrie."

"I won't."

"You could have gotten into real trouble with that nutty girl." Joe finished the last of his omelet and started on his cantaloupe. Caroline poured coffee from a thermos.

"Lillina's not nutty," she said. "She's my friend. I'm going to write to her when she goes home, and she'll write to me, and we're going to be good friends forever."

"My, my!" Joe tasted the coffee and leaned back. "Aren't we prickly today!"

"I'm not prickly," Caroline said automatically. But thinking about Lillina cast a shadow over the day. Even Mrs. Reston had cut short her scolding and fallen silent when she'd seen Lillina in the back seat of the Chevy, her expression haughty in spite of the tear streaks on her cheeks, her head high, "Like a redheaded Joan of Arc," Joe fumed after they'd driven away. "You'd think she was Mrs. Big Bucks and I was her chauffeur."

"Mrs. Reston wanted to send Lillina home right away, but now she might let her stay for a while," Caroline said. "She's going to take her to a psychiatrist, if her mother says it's okay."

"Good idea," Joe growled. "Somebody better put that kid in touch with the real world — help her to settle down."

Caroline looked out over the yard. Memories crowded around her: Lillina admiring the sandpiper in the living room; Lillina in the yellow dress; Lillina pirouetting through the darkness and calling to the moon goddess. Putting Lillina in touch with the real world was important, but Caroline decided she was glad to have known her before she "settled down." *I'm going to give her a souvenir of this summer*, she decided. *The room with the little blue rocker.*

As soon as they'd eaten, they cleared away the dishes and Joe carried the card table into the house. Caroline swept the floor of the gazebo so it would be spotless for the home-coming, and Joe brought out the yellow-flowered chaise longue he'd bought as a finishing touch.

"What do you say?" He looked around proudly. "Do you think Linda's going to like it?"

"She'll love it," Caroline assured him. And then, because it seemed as good a time as any to mention it, she said, "I have nearly enough money saved up for the trip to England this Christmas, Joe. I need about twenty dollars more, but I'll find a way to earn it this fall and — "

Joe sat down with a thump on the end of the chaise. "You what? What trip to England? What are you talking about?"

Patiently, Caroline reminded him of Jeannie's invitation and of Grandma Parks's promise to buy the airplane ticket if Caroline could earn one hundred dollars for spending money.

Joe's eyes widened under bushy brows as he listened. "That was just a lot of talk," he said heavily. "That was a daydream, Carrie. You don't really expect to — "

Keep calm. Caroline smiled at him. "Yes, I do," she said. "I'm bringing it up now so you can help me convince Mom, okay?"

He didn't answer right away, but the look

he gave her said clearly that, as far as he was concerned, good old Caroline had disappeared forever.

"We'll see," he said finally. "We'll think about it."

"Great!" That was all she'd expected, for now. Caroline looked around the gazebo that was suddenly much too small to hold her excitement. She was going to England, all by herself. She knew it, as surely as if she were already floating out over the Atlantic. And after that, there would be other adventures. She wouldn't just dream about them — she'd make them happen.

She threw open the screen door and pirouetted across the lawn.

"Caroline Cabot, you can do anything," she whispered to herself. "You really are amazingly like Eleanor."

About the Author

BETTY REN WRIGHT's short stories have appeared in *Redbook, Ladies' Home Journal, Young Miss*, and many other magazines. The author of *A Ghost in the Window, Christina's Ghost, Ghosts Beneath Our Feet, The Dollhouse Murders* (a 1983 Edgar Award nominee in the best juvenile category, and winner of the Texas Bluebonnet Award), *The Secret Window*, and *Getting Rid of Marjorie* (all Apple paperbacks), she has also written thirty-five picture books.

An enthusiastic angler, grandmother, and cat and dog owner, Ms. Wright lives in Kenosha, Wisconsin, with her husband, a painter.

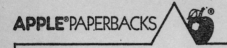